Reaper's Girl

Book #5 in the Rockin' Country Series

By Laramie Briscoe

Edited by: Lindsay Gray Hopper
Cover Art by: Kari Ayasha, Cover to Cover Designs
Proofread by: Dawn Bourgeois
Beta Read by: Keyla Handley & Danielle Wentworth
Formatting: Paul Salvette, BB eBooks
Photography by: MH Photography
Cover Models: Ashley & Jack Edmund

Wife
Husband
Parents
Entertainers

Reaper and Harmony have been enjoying being Garrett and Hannah since their respective tours ended. They've become closer, learned to live as a married couple, and been successful in keeping relevant without having their faces on the cover of tabloids. Raising their eighteen-month-old son, is the highlight of both their lives.

Now that they've settled into a routine, Hannah misses the studio, and decides to give Harmony one more shot. Because he's always been supportive, Garrett agrees. Neither one of them are prepared for the sheer popularity their marriage and the birth of their child has given them as a couple. When the album drops, it sets forth a series of events neither one of them are prepared for.

To everyone's, surprise Harmony Stewart becomes more of a household name, has a Pop number one, and gets way in over her head with commitments.

The success, the pressure, and the fame all gets to be too much. It doesn't take long to realize there's only one title she's ever wanted to have.

Reaper's Girl

Dedication

To Nicole, Carrie, Danielle, Keyla, Heather, Reva, Amanda, and anyone else Reaper & Harmony have touched. I'm super proud to be a Reaper's Girl with you ladies!

Chapter One

April

"I think it's time. I wanna go back into the studio."

Hannah Thompson glanced over to her left at her husband, who sat behind the wheel of their Range Rover. Her gaze washed over him, taking in the way he shifted against the leather of the seat, leaned back further, and spread his knees wider, taking up almost all of the room under the wheel. She didn't miss the way his green eyes flashed to the rearview mirror, gazing in the back to their son, EJ, in his booster seat. Garrett licked his lips before taking a drink of coffee from its white cup—from that place he always gave her crap about—before his eyes took in her profile.

"Is that what you want, babe?"

His deep voice calmed her, and she knew he wasn't asking for him, he was asking for her.

She nodded. "Yeah, I'm sure. He's almost a year and a half old now. I mean nobody probably even cares about me as anything more than a wife or a mom anymore."

Hannah could feel the heat of his gaze on her. "Trust me, Han, nobody thinks of you as *just* a wife or a mom."

"It's not a bad thing if they did," she was quick to defend.

He laughed loudly. "That's not it at all, but lately I'm on the internet way more than you are. I know you see your comments, but I also know you've taken a step back. Shell may not be telling you, but people are constantly asking when you're going to have something out, when I'm gonna let you out of the house."

"What?"

"Yeah, people think I'm keeping you home and that I want to keep you knocked up so you don't have a chance to go back in the studio or on the road. You know that's not the case, right? Anything you wanna do, you can do. I'm not going to hold you back from anything, but it has to be right for us as a family." He glanced back at EJ, who was now sleeping, as they made their way into downtown Nashville.

"I agree." She turned in her seat so that she could look at her husband. "Never would I want to put him in any kind of situation where he wasn't a priority. Our family always comes first, and that's why I've been hesitant to do anything."

"But you're ready now?" he asked as he checked his blind spot and exited the interstate.

Hannah took a moment. Was she really ready? Or was she bored? That was something she asked herself a lot—especially lately. EJ didn't need her as much as he had when he was a newborn, and she found herself having time that wasn't preoccupied anymore. "I think so, but my thought goes back to what do I do with him while I'm in the studio." She nodded back to EJ.

Garrett reached over and grabbed her hand. "You know we're on a break right now. We're going to be writing our record, and we have a year to do that. Do you have songs and stuff already picked out?"

"I've been listening to demos," she admitted. "The good ones Shell has been hearing, she's been forwarding my way. I've found songs I really like, and there are a few songs I've written that I think are something. I won't know until I get into the studio though."

Bringing her hand up to his lips, he grinned. "Then why don't you figure out if they're something or not? I say if this is something you wanna do—we'll make it work."

And that was exactly why she had the best husband in the world.

Chapter Two

Two Months Later

Hannah juggled the slippery plastic of the Starbucks drink she held in her hand as she used a code she hadn't used in a very long time. The June Nashville heat made condensation appear on the cup as soon as she wiped it off, but it was nothing compared to the way her palms were sweating. Her purse slipped off her shoulder, and she huffed, frustrated with herself by the way her heart was pounding at unnatural speeds.

There was no reason to be nervous. She was a Grammy winner. Going back into the studio wasn't that big of a deal. Squaring her shoulders and taking a deep breath, she glanced at her wedding ring. Garrett was supporting her the whole way; he'd sent her off this morning with EJ on his hip and breakfast in her stomach. Along with the drink she held in her hand.

"This ain't your first rodeo, Han," she told herself as she put her purse back on her shoulder, got a better grip on her cup of coffee, and opened the door.

As soon as she entered the lobby, *hellos* and *welcome*

backs were thrown at her from every direction. She smiled, knowing everyone meant it, knowing most of these people were beyond happy to see her. She was happy to see them too.

"Harmony, it's so good to see you back." The receptionist who'd been hired as Hannah had gone on maternity leave waved to her. Hannah wasn't sure of her name, so she just waved back.

"Thanks! I'm really happy to be back." And it hit her how true that statement was. She'd been afraid she'd get here and wish she was back home with Garrett and EJ, but getting out of the house was nice. "Do you know which room I'm in today?"

"You're in Studio C with Kurt."

Hannah smiled. She loved Kurt. She'd worked with him numerous times, and he'd produced most of the songs with which she'd hit number one. "Thanks, I'll be seeing you around."

She knew exactly where Studio C was, not much had changed in this place. The halls were like the well-traveled halls of a high school she'd been going to for years. The closer she got to the room, the less nervous she was, and the more excitement won out in her stomach.

There was no hesitation when she put her hand on the door and turned the knob. She opened it with a huge smile on her face.

"Hannah!" she heard from an older male voice.

Looking to her left, she saw Kurt sitting at the soundboard, but when he saw her, he got up, opening his arms.

"I'm so excited to see you," she squealed as she met him with a big hug. "When they told me I was in here with you, I was so relieved," she admitted.

"I have to tell you," he helped her with the cup of coffee as she set her purse down, "when they called me last week and told me I'd be working with you, I asked them if they were serious. I wasn't sure you'd ever be back."

"I knew I'd be back," she admitted. "But I also knew it had to be right for my family. We're at that point in our lives. It's time, because I'm getting antsy."

"Well I have to say, I'm really glad to have you back. I think as soon as people realize you've scheduled some studio time, you're gonna have more attention than you wanted."

Hannah was afraid of that; afraid of the pressure she knew came with what she did. In the past she'd crumbled under it, and at some points it had crippled her. But she was a stronger woman now, a stronger person, with the most supportive people behind her. Having her family and friends meant everything to her, and if there was anything Garrett had truly done for her, it was showing her how strong she was. With him behind her, lending a hand on her back when she needed the gentle reminder of his presence, she could do anything.

"I refuse to let people pressure me this time, but I've heard from a couple people this could be crazy."

Kurt had a seat in his chair and motioned for Hannah to have a seat across from him. "I think you underestimate the love people have for you. There's a reason you have millions of Instagram followers. People are interested in you and the love story you and Garrett have shared with the public at large. Just be aware, this could ramp it up. I don't want you to get too over-whelmed."

She took a deep breath. "I'm not going to. I know what I'm doing and I'm ready to work."

Truer words had never been spoken. She'd been so excited this morning, getting ready for her day and knowing she'd spend a few hours out of the house. It wasn't that she didn't love EJ and Garrett, or that she didn't love her role as mom and wife, but she missed Harmony. She missed being able to let that part of her personality take over and be someone new for the night, or even a few hours. Part of her even missed the stage.

"Good." Kurt grinned. "I have some songs here for you. Shell sent them over last week, and I do love what the two of you have picked out, but I know you. You've probably got a binder of original stuff too. So let's see what you got and get to work."

This is what she loved about him. He knew how she worked, respected what she wanted the process to be, and knew when to push her. "I do have a binder full of songs. Some of them I like, some I'm not sure about, but I did bring it with me."

She grabbed the bag she'd brought with her and pulled the binder out, grimacing under the weight of it.

"Holy shit, Hannah. How many songs are in here?" he laughed as he saw the width of it.

"Hundreds, if not thousands. I can't put any more in here and close it," she admitted, her face red.

"Not all of them are good." She pulled her bottom lip between her teeth. "Especially the ones I wrote right after EJ was born. I was tired and couldn't sleep most of the time, so I just wrote. I don't expect us to record those."

He gave her a glance that shut her up.

"Fuck that noise, Hannah. You know you're a good songwriter. I would venture to say you're probably better than ninety percent of what's on the radio—and that's even when you don't try."

She blushed because she still wasn't used to those comments from people in the industry.

"We'll go through it and see what you have. If it's something you feel like you wanna work on, we'll work on it." He handed the binder back to her. "Sound good?"

This was all happening so fast, faster than she'd assumed it would. But she was ready, more prepared for this than she'd ever been before. She could do this: be a wife, be a mother, be a friend, and be an amazing entertainer. There was no one holding her back but herself. It was time to step out of the shadow she'd held over herself for so long and show the world who Harmony Stewart really was.

"Sounds great." She grinned. "I know I seem shaky, but I'm really excited. Just nervous."

"Anyone in your situation would be, Hannah. When news of this gets out, and when people hear there's definitely going to be a record dropped, it'll be massive."

That was her fear. That it would be massive, or it would be crickets. Either way, she kind of wanted something in the middle. She was very well aware that she couldn't predict or generally sway the outcome of any of it, but hearing the possibility did scare her slightly.

"Whatever it is, it is, Kurt. I just wanna get started and have something to show for it by the end of the year."

"Oh, doll, we'll be done before that. You've got so much emotion and energy pent up, I say this thing will be ready for release in November. We might even hit the Grammy cut-off."

Now that was going a little too far. "Let's not get too excited." She laughed.

"So here's what we'll do. Are there any songs you've written that you absolutely love and want them to be a part of this?" he asked, eyeing her binder.

There were a few, but she'd been ready to give them up, to make room for more well-known writers. "A couple," she hedged.

"Okay, let's look at those first, then we'll move to the ones Shell forwarded over to me. If that's not enough to make an album, *then* we'll go looking. Sound like a plan?"

She smiled, breathing easily for the first time. This wouldn't be bad at all. "It does. Let's get started."

Chapter Three

Hannah entered the downtown Nashville restaurant with a huge smile on her face. As the hostess stopped her, she gave the reservation name.

"I'm meeting the Thompson party."

She was shown back to a private room, and her smile got bigger as she saw Garrett situating EJ in a kid's chair, along with Shell and Jared.

"Mama!" he yelled, holding his arms out for her.

Her heart melted as she saw EJ's face. There was nothing about the kid that didn't make her smile. She leaned in, kissing him before giving Garret a kiss on the lips. Waving at Jared and Shell, she had a seat and took a drink of the water that had already been placed in front of her.

"How did your first day at the studio go?" Garrett asked as she got settled.

"Really good. I'm with Kurt." She glanced over at Shell.

"I saw that when I looked at the info the record company sent over. That's why I didn't offer to go with you; I knew you wouldn't need me," Shell took a sip from her wine glass. "He's one of the least invasive producers around. You let me know if you need me, but I'll let you handle it for as long as you want to."

Hannah appreciated the way Shell had taken a step back in her life. The two of them had learned a few things about each other in the last year and a half, as they'd taken time off the road. They'd learned they could still be best friends and not be completely in each other's business. "I think I'll be good, but I'd like you to come in next week. He wants to talk about a marketing plan, and you're much better at that. I'm just good at keeping the fans updated."

Shell nodded, putting the information into her phone. Hannah took the moment to observe her and Jared. They'd been married for a few months, and they were still in the newlywed stage. Both of them were glowing with love, and she was so happy for them.

"What did you do today?" Garrett asked as he put an arm around her and pulled her as close as the chairs would allow them.

They were interrupted by the waiter, but this was one of their favorite spots, so they ordered their regulars and she turned to him. "Basically we went through the binder of songs I've been accumulating since I took time off. We found a couple we both really liked, and we'll be working on those this week. He wants this whole album to be me, and I agree with him as long as we can find the correct songs."

"Are you excited?" He leaned in, kissing her on the

neck.

"I'm so excited. The record company gave me carte blanche, because they didn't expect me to come back this early," she explained as she took a sip of her glass of wine. "There's a couple different ways we could go, but I'm looking forward to any of them."

"How was your day?" she asked, reaching over to hand EJ a piece of bread from the basket sitting on the table.

"We had a good day." He took a drink of his beer, putting his arm behind her chair and rubbing her neck. "EJ and I went with Jared to Crossfit. Pretty sure I puked up everything I've eaten for three days," he joked as he rubbed his side. "That shit is no joke. Give me the park and a running trail any day."

She laughed and Shell snickered.

"I can't believe you got suckered." Shell pointed at him. "I went once."

"She's a quitter." Jared put his hand over her mouth, covering up the words.

She reached and grabbed his hand so her words could be heard. "He said, 'baby, it's not that bad. It's hot, but you're in good shape, you'll be fine.'" She shot him a side-eye. "He fucking lied. Lied his ass off. I thought I was having a heart attack; you're lucky you just puked."

Since Jared had begun to take his drug recovery seriously, he'd become just as serious about his health. The rest of them were trying to keep up.

"Poor thing." Hannah glanced over at EJ. "What did he do while the two of you were Crossfitting?"

Their appetizer came and Garrett growled. "I'm so fucking hungry; I think I can eat this whole thing on my own." He grabbed a plate and got his portion. "They have one of those foam pits. He had the best time ever jumping in it. They have a kid's class. I think we should see about enrolling him. He's a little young yet, but the guy who owns the place said because of his height, he'd be okay."

EJ was taking after Garrett in the looks and height department. The only thing of hers their son had was her eyes. "It might help him get some of his energy out too." She quirked her brow.

"God, he has so much energy." Shell sighed. "I watched him while they went to lunch, after Crossfit. How did he still have that much energy?"

Hearing everyone talk about what kind of a day they'd had with her son made Hannah feel bad. She hadn't been a part of it. The past year and a half she'd been his whole day, and he'd been hers. "I'm sorry I missed all of it." Her voice was quiet.

"You were working, babe. You didn't miss anything. He was being a regular kid, and all of us were trying to keep up with him." He tipped her head up with a finger under her chin. "You're missing the fact it took three of us to take care of him, compared to just you. He was definitely pushing his boundaries, and he didn't take a nap. I'm warning you now in case he loses his shit here in a little bit."

"Garrett," she sighed, "he has to take his nap."

"You know he doesn't lay down as well for me as he

does for you. It's something we're going to have to figure out. You're gonna have to teach me your ways."

Already she was starting to feel the pressure of being a working mom. Grabbing her wine glass, she took a liberal drink, trying to tell herself there were a million women in the world who were working moms. She'd figure this out. Looking around, she realized with the help of her friends and family she'd make this work. She just hoped in the end there wouldn't be a cost. It would kill her if her son's life or her marriage suffered because of her desire to work.

"I'll see you at home." Garrett gave her a kiss as he shut the door to her SUV.

They'd had a great dinner with friends, and they were now headed home. Because they'd driven separately, they'd be going home the same way.

"See you there. Love you." She rubbed his cheek as he leaned his forehead against hers.

"Love you too, babe. We'll see ya in a few."

She watched as he got into his Range Rover, started it, and left the parking lot. Hannah put her SUV in gear and followed him onto I-65. Traffic this time of night wasn't horrible, but it sometimes still gave her a little bit of anxiety. Reaching over, she turned the radio on for the first time in a while and listened to a local station.

"News out of downtown today: word has it Harmony Stewart was seen at a local recording studio. Does this mean she's recording a new album? We're not sure, but we hope so. Country radio seriously needs her back."

They played one of her older songs as they finished speaking. She'd thought nobody would notice, nobody would care that she'd gone into the studio today, but it looked as if she was dead wrong. In her car, on her own, she wasn't sure exactly how she felt about people contemplating her next career moves. It meant expectations she'd thought she'd moved away from. But she'd sorely underestimated people's interest in her.

It wasn't enough to make her want to stop, wasn't enough to make her scared, but it was enough to make her pause. She would definitely need to talk to Garrett when she got home. She wanted to make sure he was okay with the way it looked like things were going to go.

Either way, it felt as if this was the beginning of something new and exciting. It felt like she was recording her first album again, and while that was enough to give her a little bit of anxiety, it was also enough to make her excited for it. Getting out of the house today, doing her hair and makeup, seeing other people besides her husband and toddler. It'd done her good, but she'd have to wait and see what it meant in the long run.

And right now, she realized as she pulled into her driveway, all she wanted to do was lay in bed with her husband.

Chapter Four

"Babe, I don't know how you watch him every day by yourself. I'm fucking exhausted." Garrett groaned as he plopped back into their bed.

Hannah laughed as the weight of him made her move slightly towards the middle. He captured her in his arms, and she rested her head on his chest. "I normally don't do Crossfit, maybe that's the difference."

"Nah." He shook his head. "I was exhausted before I ever tried that."

"How was he today? Any meltdowns?"

Garrett scooted up so he lay back against the headboard, taking her with him. "Only one when he realized you were leaving and not taking him with you."

She'd worried about that most of the day. EJ wasn't used to her being gone all the time. He was used to her being the one putting him down for naps and generally being the person he saw most all day.

"There's going to be some growing pains," Garrett was saying as he turned so they could face each other. "On both of our parts. I didn't know if it was okay for me to text you today or anything like that. I didn't want to interrupt your process."

"I wondered why I didn't hear from you today, but I figured it was because you were busy with him. I'm never too busy to answer a text from you. I know this is something we're going to have to get used to, me being out of the house. But honestly, I don't want to go the whole day and not hear from you."

It was weird, she realized. They were going to have to figure out how her work fit into their personal lives again. She'd grown accustomed to basically doing what she wanted when she wanted. The luxury wouldn't be there for the foreseeable future.

"We'll figure this out," his deep voice spoke into her ear.

"I hope I haven't ruined the good thing we had."

"Hannah." His tone was sharp, and he turned so that she rested underneath him, against the mattress. "Stop worrying. This is going to be fine. You're scared because you haven't done the recording and performing thing in a long time, but trust me when I say this is going to be fine."

She worried that it wouldn't be, that something would happen and it would ruin the groundwork they'd laid in their marriage.

"Stop thinking," he told her. "Stop thinking about all the things that can go wrong. Enjoy the moment."

"I can't," she admitted. "I had fun today, and it was nice to be in the studio, but as soon as I saw y'all tonight, I started to get scared and anxious."

Hannah wished she were different, but this is who she was; this was how she handled things. Frustrated when tears came to her eyes, she closed them and willed her heart to slow down. This was only day one. How was she going to feel on day nineteen? Would she back out? What had gone so wrong?

Garrett knew if he didn't get Hannah out of her own head fast, she'd derail everything she'd been excited about when she'd told him about wanting to go back into the studio. Having her underneath him was all the motivation he needed to begin that distraction.

"Do you think I've made the wrong decision?" she asked, her eyes bright with worry and what looked like tears.

"What?" He shook his head. "Fuck no, Han."

She cut him off. "You know I hate that word."

A wicked grin came to his face. She may hate that word, but she damn sure loved the act. Grasping her around the wrists with his strong hands, he pushed her arms up over her head.

"What are you doing?" she asked, although as he situated himself on top of her, he noticed her legs parted pretty quickly.

"I think you know, babe."

The way her lips parted and her heartbeat increased against his chest told him she did know, and maybe she wanted it too. Somewhere in the back of his mind, he thought sometimes she protested so much because she wanted him to take the decision away from her—and that was fine with him. He lived to dominate her in ways designed to make her body sing.

"We're having a conversation," she gave a half-hearted protest.

Moving his head down her torso as he held her hands firmly, he used his other hand to push her tank top up and over her chest. For long minutes he gazed at her bare skin, watching as her nipples tightened and her breasts lifted against his gaze.

"Are we?" he questioned.

Before she could answer, he captured a hard nub in his mouth, hollowing his cheeks as he gave her what he knew she wanted. He loved the way her fingers gripped his, the way her fingernails dug into his wrists, the way her lower body thrust against his. What was even better was knowing no other man would ever get to experience the vault of passion he'd opened when he'd been gifted with her. People made fun of how goody-goody she was all the time. Lots of his friends in the industry questioned why a guy like him would want to be with a woman like her. More times than he cared to count, they'd hit him in the side and make a joke about him probably having to do it with the lights off every night. He grinned, indulged in their joke, but he knew what he was living with, knew what he had in his arms every night, and goddamn did he love to make her want it.

"Garrett," she breathed, pushing her lower body against his.

"Thought we were talking," he mumbled as he pulled

away from her skin and released her wrists.

Once they were free, he pushed the tank top completely over her head and threw it on the floor. They worked together to take off her panties, and as he layered himself over her body again, he growled when her hands pushed down the back of his boxer briefs.

He pushed his mouth into her neck, focusing on the point that made her squirm every time he found it. The trick was to get Hannah out of her own head, but she was sneaky too. Her nails dug into the flesh of his ass as he flexed at her.

Garrett loved the way she showed him, even if she couldn't always tell him, what she wanted. One hand left his ass cheek and curled around his neck, holding him tightly to her.

"I love you," she whispered as she began thrusting up against him.

It was a special kind of torture. The fact she was completely naked and he still had underwear on. He could feel her heat, her wetness, against his cotton fabric, but he didn't want to stop long enough to push them the rest of the way down. She was thrashing her head as he worked the column of her throat. He could feel the hard pebbles of her nipples against his chest and the bite of her nails in his neck.

His voice was guttural as the words were pulled from his throat. "Push 'em down, pull it out, and put me inside of you."

He felt her mouth open as her jaw hit his forehead. He loved that sharp intake of breath when he surprised her with something he said. As he worked her skin, he waited to see if she would follow his lead. When she did, he thought he was going to come out of his skin. His ab muscles quivered as her small hands worked down his stomach, pushing the elastic band down, so she could reach inside and grasp his length.

He pushed himself up on his arms and grunted at the effort it took, because they were still like jelly from his earlier workout. Letting his head fall forward on his shoulders, he dipped his head and used his tongue to swipe against one of the nipples he loved so much. Groaning, he felt her hand push against him in an up and down motion and he thrust his hips towards her.

"Go, babe." He leveraged himself up, capturing her lips with his.

She opened her mouth for him, just like she opened herself up to him, and guided him into her body. They both moaned, her hands clasping at him, his hands gripping the sheets as he worked himself into her heat.

Their tongues dueled as he started rocking into her, pulling his mouth from hers when her legs wrapped around his waist, holding him closer. "You're so fucking hot," he breathed into her ear, dropping one elbow to the mattress.

"You're so hard." She pushed her head back against the pillow, giving him free reign to her flesh. "Feels so good."

He had to agree; everything he did with her always felt good. There was no faking with either one of them; they knew how to play each other's bodies like well-loved instruments. Fast or slow, it didn't matter.

As he felt her body tighten, he pushed a knee to the mattress to gain more leverage, and as he felt her let go, he whispered the one thing he knew she loved.

"I got you."

Chapter Five

"Try it again, Hannah," Kurt cut in when she didn't quite hit the note like he wanted her to.

When she tried again, he stopped her one more time. "You're not getting it, Han. I need you to put feeling into it. I need you to sing like the thing you love most in the world is right in front of you."

She fought back the tears that pricked at her eyes. They'd been working on this section of the song for over two hours, and it *was not* coming. This was the hard part, trying to make something happen and force it when she just didn't have it in her.

"Don't get upset, Hannah," he tried to talk her down from the booth.

She cleared her throat, hoping her frustration didn't show, but she knew it would. "It's right there, I just can't get to the emotion. I feel it…" She trailed off.

"Why don't you do this? Why don't you take thirty, come back, and we'll try it again? Having a hard day in the studio isn't the end of the world. We've had some very good ones. This is a bump in the road."

He was right, and she knew it. Not everything came perfectly the first time around, the second, or even in her case the fifteenth tonight, but she was a professional, and this was frustrating. "Okay, give me thirty to forty-five minutes. I'll come back with a better mindset." She hoped.

Grabbing her purse and phone, she walked out to her SUV before getting in and placing a call to Garrett. He didn't answer and that disappointed her more than she could say. Trying again, she hit the FaceTime button, but again, it went unanswered. It was then that everything hit her, and she leaned forward, resting her head against the steering wheel as she sobbed her frustration. He was the one person who would be able to get her through this, he was the one she wanted to talk to more than anyone else, and he wasn't answering. Having been home with EJ by herself though, she knew it was difficult to take care of a toddler on your own, and more than likely he was paying attention to their son, but it didn't stop the tears from coming. It felt good to release the frustration and tension, so she let them flow. Hannah was having a pity party—party of one—and she was really okay with that.

Finally, the shakes stopped, the tears stopped, and she glanced at the clock. She still had fifteen minutes, and with the splitting headache she now had, caffeine was a must. A Starbucks was right up the road, and she knew she could hit their drive-thru quickly.

Fifteen minutes later with drink in hand, she made her way back into the studio, still not sure if she could do what Kurt was asking her to. When she opened the door and walked in, she was greeted with the best present ever.

"Here she is. I figured she'd be back soon," she heard Kurt say.

EJ scrambled down off Garrett's lap and ran for his mom, hugging her tightly around the legs before she could set her stuff down. When she finally did, she picked him up, hugging him tightly against her, kissing his cheek. "What are you doing here?"

"We were in the area and figured we'd come see how work was going," Garrett answered, smiling his wide smile at her. He was in workout clothes, so he must have been running in the park up the road with Jared.

"I'm glad you're here. I tried to call and FaceTime you."

He lifted his phone up. "I saw, but I didn't have the Bluetooth connected and I was driving. Kurt told me what happened."

She bit her lip, nodding. She didn't want to seem like she didn't have it all together with Garrett sitting right there in front of her.

Kurt looked back and forth between the two of them before he slapped his thighs. "Hey EJ, there's popsicles in the break room. You like popsicles?"

"Orange?" he asked, clear as day. He did love his orange popsicles.

"I'm sure we could wrangle up an orange one while your mom and dad talk. Wanna come with me?"

He glanced at his mom. "Go?"

"You can go with Mr. Kurt. Be sure and pay attention to him and don't run off." She sat him on his feet and pulled his shirt down, making sure he looked presentable.

"We'll be back," Kurt told them as he grabbed EJ's small hand in his.

She watched as they left and then turned to Garrett.

"Wanna talk about it?" he asked as he held his arms out to her, moving his thighs apart so he could make room for her there.

"I just…" She shook her head, not sure of the words she wanted to say. What *was* there really to say? "I can't seem to make this happen today."

"You got this, Han. Why are you holding yourself back?"

That was the question of the last three hours. Why was she holding herself back? Why wouldn't she let the emotions go? "I guess," she shrugged and then bit her lip, sighing, "I don't want to sing this song without you here. I wrote it for you, and it feels weird without you here."

"Well, I'm here now, and you can make this song your bitch."

She giggled, leaning in to give him a kiss on the lips. "And I miss you."

"Miss you too, babe. That's kinda why we're here today. EJ was asking for you, and I really was right down the road, so we decided to stop in. I hoped you wouldn't be mad and Kurt wouldn't be mad, but he looked relieved when I walked in."

"I bet he was," she agreed. "I think he was getting as frustrated with me as I was with myself."

"Sometimes it happens."

They were pulling apart when Kurt and EJ walked back in.

"Are you ready?" he asked her, eating a popsicle of his own.

"I am."

"Go on." He motioned to the sound booth. "Go in there and show me what you can do."

Squaring her shoulders, she walked in, knowing her husband and son were sitting right outside. She watched as Garrett picked EJ up and sat him on his lap. With her eyes on his, she did just as asked; she showed them all what she could do.

Chapter Six

"So how are you handling it?"

Garrett looked up from the green numbers of the treadmill he was on to glance at his best friend's face. They'd forgone Crossfit today and had decided to make use of their gym membership.

"Handling what?"

Jared gave an exasperated sigh. "We're three weeks into Hannah recording this album. How are you handling it? Jesus, I have to spell everything out for you."

The question was a popular one with anyone who knew the two of them. He'd been asked the same thing more than he cared to admit. Everyone assumed he was so broken up over the fact she'd decided to go back to work that no one listened to what he actually said.

"I'm doing good. EJ, on the other hand, has been having a hard time, which makes me a little stressed. It is what it is though, and there's no way in hell I'm asking Hannah to give up something she wants to do because our son's being a brat." He hit the treadmill harder as he spoke.

"You sure about what you're saying? You're running awfully hard over there."

Garrett was pissed, but not how most people assumed. While her decision affected his life and EJ's life, most people seemed to forget how much it affected Hannah's as well. Returning to the studio wasn't something she'd taken lightly. She'd worried about it, stewed over it, and asked his opinion thousands of times before she'd actually pulled the trigger on getting the record company behind her. For so many to assume he made her decisions for her chapped his ass (and now he was thinking like his father-in-law spoke). He realized how hard his feet were slapping against the belt of the treadmill and stepped off, while he tried to get his breathing under control.

"I'm sure. It's not her being in the studio that's pissing me off. It's everybody else's assumptions."

Jared glanced at his friend, concern on his face. "What assumptions?"

"If I've ever heard or read it once, it's been a million times. Industry types want to say I've been keeping her to myself because I can't stand to be with a woman who's more popular than me and my band. Do you know what a load of bullshit that is? I'm proud of her, more proud than I've ever been, because I know how hard this was for her. I was the person who listened to her and still listens to her second-guess herself every day, and it feels like all these article writers just want to see her fail. Jared, if she fails it's going to ruin her. Do you understand me? Ruin her." He ran a hand through his hair, pushing out breath from his tight lungs. "I want to make a statement and rip out the jugular of every asshole who assumes what they want about our relationship and my reaction to her going back to work, but then I feed into all of it, and where are we? Back at fucking square one."

"This is really bothering you?" Jared phrased it as a question.

"It's fucking me up, because if I say something, I look like a dick. If I don't say anything, I look like a dick, and in the end, I feel like, no matter what, the person who gets hurt the most is Hannah."

Jared ran a hand over his beard-covered face. "Is she even aware of what's going on?"

Garrett shook his head. "Not really. You know as well as I do, she basically leaves social media to Shell. I mean she posts on it, but she doesn't read the comments, not anymore."

"Then let it ride out, man. No matter what it's going to get worse before it gets better. You and I both know that. If she's oblivious, then good on her, and you don't have to worry about her freaking out."

He could understand what his friend was saying, but he still wanted to be the person to protect his wife. She didn't deserve any of this. "It's hard as hell for me to keep my mouth shut and not tell them to fuck off."

"Which is why you're telling me all your issues," Jared reasoned. "We've been in this game long enough to know what's acceptable and what's not. You keep your mind good for her, and I'll listen to you bitch. It's what friends do."

Two years ago, Garrett realized this conversation wouldn't be happening. Jared had been relapsing from a drug addiction, and they'd had to take a step back from their friendship so he could get the help he'd needed. Now, more than ever, Garrett was thankful to have his best friend back in his life. "I'm glad you're here."

"I'm reading between the lines." Jared grimaced. "And I have to say I'm glad I'm here too. Things have changed for both of us in the past few years, in ways we never thought."

Laughing as he got back on his treadmill, Garrett shook his head. "We're both married, I'm a dad. Back when we first met Hannah, it wasn't even a blip on my radar. Sure I was sick of everything, but I never assumed or thought I'd settle down so quickly."

"Do you ever miss it? The way life used to be, before we started wearing these?" Jared lifted up his left hand so his friend could see his wedding ring. He was quiet for a long time, and Jared actually worried what the answer was going to be.

"No." His voice was firm with the answer. "I've never missed it since Hannah came into my life. Do I sometimes wish I didn't have so much responsibility? Fuck yes. Ya know raising a kid is a huge deal. I feel like I have to set a good example all the time, and we both can remember me being a teenager and a young guy who rebelled against anything or anyone trying to make me do good things for myself." He stopped speaking and checked the screen on his phone. It held a picture of his family. "But I don't regret for one minute asking Hannah to marry me, agreeing to have a child, and giving up the life of different women every night. I love our life together, I love being settled. I just wish everyone else would shut the fuck up."

That was the one thing he and Hannah had wished from the moment they'd gone public with their relationship.

"I don't think I've ever been so happy to see the ass-end of a week in my life."

Hannah laughed as she and Kurt packed up the room they'd been using to record. In the past few weeks they'd chosen songs, laid down some tracks, and now they were getting to the rough parts of the job. They were starting to do the fine-tuning, ad-libbing, and making the hard decisions. She had to agree this week had been a hard one on them. They'd butted heads a few times, but he'd respected her opinion and listened as she explained her position before he explained his. A few times she'd not accepted what he'd thought, and other times she'd agreed. It was a much different experience than any of the other ones she'd ever had before. It was new, exciting, and in many ways it felt like her first album all over again.

"I know, this week has been killer. I'm just glad Garrett agreed to put EJ down tonight so we could stay here and finish this up. We have big plans for the weekend."

She grinned.

"I imagine being married to Reaper, your house gets a little wild."

"You would think so, wouldn't you?" She raised an eyebrow as she grabbed her empty Starbucks cup and threw it away. "We're gettin' wild this weekend, lemme tell ya. Because I've missed so much with EJ, we're going to the zoo tomorrow. Shell and Jared will probably come with us, because they always come with us. We're having a family cookout tomorrow night, and then we're having a very lazy Sunday. If that's not partying it up, I don't know what is."

Kurt let out a breath. "If people only knew how domesticated your husband has become."

"Oh." She laughed. "Don't let that fool you. He's still got a very rebellious, wild side, but he can keep it under control now." Her cheeks heated up as she thought of the wild side she loved so much. Maybe she could get him to indulge in that side if she played her cards right. Mind made up, she gave herself a secretive smile. Having her husband was a pleasure only she got to experience.

"Well either way, have a great weekend." Kurt tossed her a wave as he opened the door for her.

"You too. Don't take this the wrong way," she said as she exited, looking forward to spending the weekend with her family. "It'll be nice not to have to see you for the next few days."

"The feeling is completely mutual, and I know you'll be ready to go on Monday."

There was no doubt about it. Now that Hannah had tapped into Harmony again, it felt like a piece of her was back, and she wasn't sure if she'd be able to put it back in its box again.

Chapter Seven

Hannah glanced at the numbers shining from the dashboard of her SUV. Ten o'clock was much later than she was used to. It'd been a very long time since she'd been out working this late at night, but both she and Garrett had agreed she'd stay as long as she needed to—in order to get it done. They wanted the entire weekend together so they could spend it with EJ. Family time was the most important thing to them, and if they had to sacrifice some through the week in order to have the whole weekend, they were willing to.

Parking in the garage, she turned off the engine, grinning when she saw the kitchen light on through the garage entrance. Garrett had been so good about leaving lights on for her, and generally taking care of not only her but their lives as well. He'd stepped up in a way she hadn't expected but loved just the same. Grabbing her bag, she got out and walked through and into the kitchen. Havock met her at the door with a sniff of her hand. She leaned down, giving him a pat on the nose before she walked further into the room. Her stomach growled loudly as her nose picked up the scent of her favorite pizza.

"How did you know I'd be hungry?" she asked as she set her stuff down on the counter, smiling when she saw a sleepy-looking Garrett.

"Hey, babe," he greeted her with his arms wide open.

She sank into them, loving the way they wrapped around her body, holding her close to him. He was warm and smelled like her favorite soap. Since Black Friday was taking a hiatus, he'd also taken a hiatus with his razor, and the scratchy five-o'clock shadow rubbing against her forehead made her heart race.

"Hey, were you asleep?" The space below his eyes were shadowed, and his voice was deep in the way she knew he'd at least been halfway dozing.

"In and out," he admitted, leaning down to give her a quick kiss. "We had a busy day running errands and stuff. So when I finally got him to bed, I was planning on waiting up for you, but I woke up as you were coming in the back door."

"It's okay." She knew exactly what he meant by the days being busy. She remembered with great detail how she'd woken up every day—a new list to do—and then after putting EJ to bed, she'd just wanted to collapse. "Did you order pizza?"

"Yeah, I figured you'd be hungry, and I was starving earlier."

"Let me go get changed." She was dying to get into comfortable clothes. "Then will you eat with me?"

She asked it in a small voice, kind of afraid he'd say

no, since she'd woken him up.

"You don't even have to ask, babe. Go get changed, I'll be right here." He grabbed her around the waist, pulling her back to his front and dropping a kiss on her neck.

She sighed, melting into his arms. All was right at the end of the day as long as she came home to him.

Garrett went around the kitchen, grabbing Hannah a glass of wine and sticking two pieces of pizza on a plate for her. He knew her well enough to know she liked it cold, and she liked a little minced garlic on it. Setting the container of garlic out, he grabbed himself a beer and another plate—he'd eaten earlier but only enough to make his stomach stop growling. If at all possible, he wanted to share every minute of the day they could—together.

He'd just finished setting it all out and giving Havock some extra food when she appeared in the doorway.

"I looked in on EJ, he's sleeping like a log. What'd you do with him today?" She walked over to the fridge and leaned to look in.

Standing with his back to the sink, he tilted his head to get a good look at the curve of her ass showing through the shorts she wore. "Not that I'm not loving the show you're giving me, babe, but what are you looking for?"

Turning her gaze over her shoulder, she gave him a wink. "The garlic, I can't eat pizza without garlic."

Motioning towards the table with his chin, he never took his eyes off her. "Already over there, but please keep giving me a show for as long as you want."

He watched as she gave her hips a little shake before getting upright, shutting the door, and walking over to the kitchen table. "Look at you, even got me a glass of wine. Are you being nice for a reason?"

"I'm always nice." He pushed off the counter and pulled out her chair for her. "There's never an ulterior motive, other than to get you relaxed."

"You might think I don't, but I see right through you, Reaper," she teased as she took a drink from her wine glass.

"Please enlighten me, babe."

He couldn't help the way his smile broke across his face, making his dimples pop. He loved teasing her, loved the ease of conversation the two of them had. As much as he loved his son too, there was something special about the time they spent alone together. They'd worked hard to make themselves a priority when everyone else had tried to pull them apart.

"I think," she took another drink of her wine glass, watching as he put garlic on his pizza too, "you're putting garlic on your pizza and buttering me up because you want some time alone with me. I kind of think we have a date with the couch and a movie on as background noise."

His wife had him. That was exactly what he was hoping for. "Maybe a scary one so you'll cling extra tight."

"If you play your cards right, it won't even have to be scary."

Garrett's eyebrows rose. There were different facets to Hannah's personality, and this straight shooter was a new one, but he liked it. "I keep my deck close to my chest." He wiped his mouth with his napkin as he finished his food.

He watched as she did the same before draining her wine glass. "What would you do if I said queens were wild?" She stood from her chair, walked over, and grabbed his hand, pulling him up from where he sat.

"I'd ask how wild my queen wanted to be."

"How about you let her show you?"

Garrett groaned. He was completely on board with whatever she wanted to get into tonight.

Hannah's heart pounded against her rib cage. It wasn't very often she wanted to take charge, but tonight she wanted to show him how much she appreciated everything he'd done for them. She knew it hadn't been easy for him to take up where she'd left off. He'd done it though, and not even uttered one word of protest. Hannah was grateful, because she'd gotten such a great partner in life.

"Have a seat." She took his hand over her head and sat him down on their couch.

If there was one thing she'd missed, it was the close-ness they'd adapted to while she'd been off. More than anything, she missed the quiet nights with him in front of the television. She was different than he was. When she got home from the studio, she needed to decompress, needed to have quiet for a little while. He'd been able to go headlong into family life with her and EJ when their roles had been reversed, and she hadn't realized how hard it had been for him.

Garrett raised his eyebrows at her as she went down to her knees on the soft rug they'd laid over the hardwood once EJ had started walking. It wasn't often she did this, but he'd always enjoyed it, and she enjoyed herself when she allowed her insecurities to go away. Tonight she was determined to do that. She wanted to say thank you for all the support he'd given her, but more than anything, she wanted to feel as close to him as she had before she'd started going back to work.

"You sure about this, Han?" he asked, cupping her jaw in the palm of his hand. "You have nothing to prove to me, you have nothing to thank me for. I'm supporting you. I'm your husband, that's what I'm here for."

"I know." She cleared her throat. "But that doesn't mean I can't express to you in a way we'll both enjoy just how much I appreciate it. Right?"

He ground his back teeth together as she reached up and ran her hands down his bare abdomen until she encountered the waistband of his shorts. She loved the way his stomach clenched, the way the moan sounded as if it was ripped from the back of his throat. As she slipped her hands beneath the material, all she heard was a whispered,

Fuck me.

Chapter Eight

Hannah felt powerful as she leaned over Garrett's waist, holding him steady with her hand as she enveloped him between her lips.

"Son of a bitch."

She loved to hear whatever would tumble out of his mouth when she decided to give him this pleasure. To her, this was the same thing as him treating her like a groupie. While she liked him to be in control, she was also becoming more comfortable in her role so that she could also exert control. It turned her on in ways nothing else ever had.

Squeezing her thighs together, she balanced on her knees as she dipped down again, taking him further down her throat. Using the flat of her tongue, she licked up the underside and swirled around the head, loving the vibration of his body against hers.

His fingers tangled in her hair, holding her closer as he lightly thrust into her mouth. She stopped, breathing through her nose until she was comfortable, and then took him back down, moving along with the rhythm he set.

"Damn, babe," he growled.

She looked up at him, not removing her mouth from his hard length, watching as he disentangled his hands and put his arms on the back of the couch. She watched as his big palms curled around the back and used it for leverage as he lifted up, pushing himself further into her throat.

Hannah used one hand to stroke the length she couldn't get inside her mouth and then used the other to cup his balls, squeezing gently. She'd always been shy about doing that, but she and Shell had gotten into a conversation the other day, and Shell had convinced her it was okay and Garrett would love it. Judging by the way he moaned and threw his head back against the couch, he seemed to really enjoy it.

When she couldn't breathe anymore, she lifted off his length and gasped.

She watched as Garrett's chest heaved and he breathed out a long sigh, his mouth forming the most perfect "O" she'd ever seen in her life. He rubbed his hands down his ab muscles and then flexed them against his knees. "I don't know where the fuck you learned what you're doing, but keep doing it, Han. Jesus Christ," he whined again as he took him back into her mouth.

It wasn't very often she saw him lose control at her ministrations. Normally Garrett let her come first, always made sure she was taken care of, and then he'd let himself go. Tonight though, she wanted this, she wanted his orgasm more than she wanted hers. Gathering her wits about her, she took him down her throat, pausing slightly to adjust, and then swallowed against the girth.

"Fucking hell, woman," he gasped, his eyes popping open, mouth gaping.

He watched her like he had no idea who she was, and it made her want to giggle, that this far into their relationship she could still surprise him.

Who was this woman and what had she done with his wife? Innocent? Not anymore. He'd done a great job of corrupting her from their dating days, and he couldn't help but be proud of not only himself but her too. Back then she'd had a shell around her body, scared to admit who she really was, scared to let him in, to let herself feel too much. Somehow he'd managed to break through, and he was glad every damn day he'd not given up. Many times he could have, and nobody would have blamed him. What resulted now was the most pure, uncompromising love he'd ever experienced.

Twining his fingers through her dark hair, he pulled her mouth back, but she fought against his grip, not wanting to let go. The force tightened the strands against her head, and she moaned against the pressure he exerted.

"Like that?" He forced the words between gritted teeth. There wasn't much about her that didn't turn him on. Even now, he had goosebumps all over his body, running up and down his arms, his nipples were hard, and his balls were drawn up tight. She knew how to work him, and fuck if he didn't love it.

Finally slipping her mouth off his length, she directed her gaze towards him. "Yeah."

The husky quality of her voice, the stretched appearance of her lips, the half-lidded eyes she fixed on him with were enough to wreck the control he had over himself. "You want me to come?"

He wanted it so bad, but he wanted her to make the decision. It was killing him to hold back, taking everything he had, but he'd do it for her. He'd do it to let her bask in her independence. She'd started this encounter, and he wanted to be everything she had dreamed of, wanted her to walk away from it feeling like she'd accomplished everything she wanted.

Hannah nodded, swallowing so hard her throat muscles bobbed before she bent over again, taking him down in one slip of her mouth over the head of his dick.

It was the best and worst kind of torture he'd ever been subjected to in his life. Garrett loved the warmth of her mouth, the resistance when he slightly hit the back of her throat, the way she enthusiastically hollowed out her cheeks for him, and fucking appreciated the way she got her hands involved with his balls. This wasn't the same Hannah he'd met years ago, and it still struck him stupid how much she'd changed. How much she'd blossomed and grown in the strength of their relationship just with him giving her his patience. All those other people who'd made assumptions about her? He knew he was the luckiest bastard in the world.

Garrett thrust his hips against her mouth. Taking his

other hand off the back of the couch, he circled it around the base of his cock. It felt good as he tightened his grip, slipping his palm up the small portion she couldn't fit in her mouth.

"Keep going, babe," he whispered, giving her the encouragement he knew she needed.

With one hand in her hair, one hand around his cock, and her mouth encompassing him in a heat they'd built together to drive him wild, they worked in tandem to get him there.

He threw his head back against the couch, closing his eyes as he immersed himself in the sounds of the room. She slurped against his skin; his fist beat a rhythm echoing against the quietness of the house.

"Fuck." He breathed loudly, feeling himself let go against her lips. It seemed to last forever, another wave taking over his cock as he felt himself bump the back of her throat again. He did his best not to shove himself against her, but damn it felt better than anything had in a long time. "Shit, babe." He pushed deeper into her mouth before pulling out and throwing his body against the couch cushions, slumping as he tried to wipe the sweat out of his eyes.

She sat back on her knees, shoulders shaking as she wiped her mouth, her eyes meeting his. There was a heat there, but also something that looked like mischief.

"Are you okay?" he asked, putting a hand up to his chest, trying to slow his pounding heart.

She glanced up at him, a huge smile on her face as she wiped her hand on her shirt. If anyone could see her now, they would swear this wasn't her, this was someone else, but they'd become much more comfortable with each other and within their marriage. "It's in my hair."

He laughed loudly, pride washing over his face. "Oh my God, I'm so sorry." But really he wasn't, she'd blown his fucking mind, and he'd come fucking hard.

"It's okay." She giggled. If this had happened back when they'd first started dating, she wasn't sure how she would have dealt with it, but today she was happy with herself. To make her usually in control husband completely and utterly lose control? Heady stuff. "But can we take this to the shower?"

He stood up, tucking himself back in his shorts as he pulled them back up his thighs. Reaching down, he grabbed her hand and grasped her body so she had to wrap her legs around his waist. His big hands gripped her ass as he pulled her against him. Tilting his head to the side, he captured her lips in a kiss so hot they were clawing at each other again. It wasn't weird to taste himself on her tongue. It'd been happening more often than not. If anything it got him hotter for her. The fact she'd lost that inhibition with him was such a turn on. Feeling her grind against him, he pulled back, his dark eyes meeting hers. When he spoke the words, he knew they were true in every part of their lives.

"We can take this anywhere you wanna go."

Chapter Nine

Hannah woke up the next morning, a smile on her face turning into a frown as she noticed Garrett was already out of bed. It was unusual for him to be out of bed before her, but their hours were all messed up since she'd gone back into the studio. He was normally the late riser and the one to go to bed last. In essence, she'd become him, and he'd become her. A look at the clock told her she'd slept a little later than she'd wanted to, but she'd been tired once they came to bed. It had been well after one in the morning when they'd finally gotten enough of each other. And even after weeks in the studio, she was still trying to get used to what was now their new normal.

Getting up, she put her feet on the floor, wincing as she felt a soreness in her thighs. Garrett had contorted her in shapes she hadn't been in in a long time. A grin was prominent on her face though. They'd needed last night. She hadn't realized how much she missed being with him every day. Just the few hours they'd spent together was enough to remind her why they'd been together for so long. Grabbing a pair of sweatpants and one of Garrett's shirts, she quickly got dressed and made her way downstairs. The scene that greeted her made her heart happy.

Garrett and EJ lay on the couch, EJ curled up against his dad's chest, watching cartoons. They had a blanket draped over them, and Garrett looked to be asleep.

"Hey," she whispered as she entered the living room, trying to be quiet. There was no telling what time their son had woken his dad up. Chances were, Garrett had taken one for the team, to let her sleep longer.

His little voice warmed her soul as she heard him shout at her. "Mama!" No matter what, EJ was always excited to see her, and it was one of her favorite parts of being his mom.

"Shhhh," she shushed their son, a finger to her lips.

"I'm up," Garrett's sleepy voice answered from where he laid, his eyes still closed. His arm let go of EJ, and he turned onto his back, putting his arm up at an angle against the couch.

Garrett was sexy even when he all he did was sleep. She walked over to where they lay, sitting on the opposite end of the couch, grabbing the blanket to cover her feet up. EJ got up from where he lay against Garrett and crawled over to her.

"Did you sleep good?" she asked as she situated him against her, putting his head in the crook of her arm. Breathing in deeply, she smelled little boy. She loved the shampoo he used, the bubble bath he loved, and the way the smell of fabric softener and dryer sheets clung to his skin.

This was what she missed every morning when she went to the studio. The family time, the feeling of not having to run to get everything done throughout the day. What she longed for on those long days when she wasn't sure she did anything right. There had been moments that were tense, where she wasn't sure she'd done the right thing. Even when things went perfectly, sometimes the record company was still pissed at her; sometimes they still wanted her to make changes she wasn't comfortable with. It sucked all the way around. But this morning with her family? This was exactly what she needed.

"You're quiet this morning." Garrett gave her a sleepy smile, scratching his whisker-covered chin. She absolutely loved when he went a few days without shaving. He looked edible when he got lazy.

"Just enjoying my time with my favorite guys." She bent her head down to kiss EJ on the forehead before she reached over and grabbed Garrett's hand. It felt good when he caressed her knuckles, his big thumb spanning two of them at once.

"Hey, EJ." Garrett sat up, rubbing his eyes, a yawn cracking his jaw. "Guess what we're doing today."

Their toddler looked between the two of them, a bewildered expression on his face. It almost looked as if he wanted to shout something out, but he was unsure if it was correct or not. Instead, he continued looking between them.

"Remember what we've been talking about all week?

What sound do the elephants make?" Garrett started making a sound that was reminiscent of something dying, but EJ squealed immediately.

"Zoo!"

His voice was so excited it brought smiles to both of their faces.

"Yeah, the zoo." Garrett reached out to give him a high five. "Aunt Shell and Uncle Jared are coming today too. It's gonna be a good time, right?"

EJ was positively vibrating as he climbed down off the couch. His mom's arms were forgotten, hanging out with his dad was forgotten, and the TV no longer held the child's attention. He was ready to go.

"I think he's excited." Hannah laughed as she got up, grabbing hold of Garrett's hand as he held it out to her. "What exactly was that noise you made? Didn't sound like an elephant to me; it sounded like something dying. Was that the best you could come up with?"

He rolled his eyes as she helped him off the couch, letting him take her against his chest. For a moment they enjoyed each other's company, and he squeezed her tight. "No back talk about how bad my animal sounds are. Sometimes I have to improvise."

She pinched his side. "He's gonna learn the wrong thing," she protested. "When it's time for pre-school he'll probably think a dog meows and a cat barks if we leave it up to you."

He put his hand over her mouth. "Morning." He leaned down, giving her a kiss. The heat they shared silenced her protests about his teaching prowess. Instead, she leaned back against his arms around her waist. "You ready for the zoo?"

"My thighs are a little sore today, but I think I can manage."

He clasped his hands on her ass, gripping firmly as he leaned into her ear. His voice was almost ragged as he recalled the thing she'd done to him. "Your thighs? You sucked my soul out through my dick, babe."

Her face flamed hot. Even after the years they'd been together, she still wasn't used to how crass he could be. At the same time, she loved it. He didn't make everything lovey-dovey, and whether she liked to admit it or not, that kind of made her feel like a badass. Nobody ever expected the things she did with her husband of Harmony Stewart, and knowing they had their own little secrets was the most arousing thing of all.

"Let's go get dressed and call the crew. We want to get there as early as we can." She leaned up, kissing him on the cheek.

He grasped her wrist as she tried to pull away, stopping her. "What?" she asked as she looked into his eyes, not sure what she saw there. Most times he was an open book, but others he could still hold back, especially when he wanted to be serious.

"I love you, Han," he whispered as he drew her as close to him as he could get her. "I saw the way you held EJ, and I saw the look on your face. He's not missing a damn thing because you're working. I promise you. He's fine. We'll all be fine."

She let him pull her into his arms, breathing in his

scent. At times she loved and hated how he could read her like an open book; how he knew her fears so well she didn't even have to speak them. Melting into his arms, she let him take those fears away. She hoped he was telling the truth. Her plans had never included EJ feeling left out, and maybe she was projecting how she felt onto their son. Either way, she'd shake it off and make sure they had the best day ever with EJ and their friends.

Chapter Ten

"We beat most of the crowd," Jared observed as he and Shell sat in the back of the Range Rover with EJ. "Give me a high-five, dude." He put his palm up to EJ who smacked it, with a toothy grin to his uncle.

"At least we don't have to park out in no man's land." Hannah grinned as she looked back at her son. "Are you ready for the zoo?"

He'd been once before a few months ago and he'd loved it. They'd been promising to take him since. For a moment, she glanced at him. Recently he'd lost the baby fat he'd had in his cheeks, and he was starting to grow taller, filling out, and becoming leaner. She had a feeling his second birthday in a few months was going to be much harder than his first had been.

"Yes!" he answered, his face showing her all she needed to see. The excitement there was palpable. No matter how busy she'd been during the week and how much she worried EJ would feel neglected, she knew she would make sure his weekends were fun as they could be.

The group poured out and walked around to the back of the SUV. "It's gonna be a hat day," Garrett said as he rummaged through the trunk area and came up with a hat. He plopped on his head.

"You need to get that shit cut." Jared gave him a hard time, throwing a hand into Garrett's stomach.

Garrett doubled over, making an *umph* noise. "I'm thinking I might grow it out for this era of the band."

Hannah, who'd been half-way listening to their conversation as she and Shell got sunscreen on EJ and him into his stroller, turned around, her eyebrows high. "You're thinkin' *what?*"

He offered her the smile that told her he was trying to soothe ruffled feathers. "I'm thinking I might grow it out for this era of the band we'll be embarking on in the next year. It might be the last time I'm able to do it. I'm in my early thirties and all."

She gave him a skeptical look. His hair was already getting long; the ends curled against the hat he wore. It wouldn't take much for it to be down his neck. "We'll see how it looks," she said, but her voice wasn't confident.

"I'll be hot, baby, just like I am now. You remember how much you liked Jax Teller with long hair? Need I remind you?"

The group cracked up. She'd been so torn up when his TV show had ended. "Need I remind *you* my favorite look for him was when he came out of prison in season four and he was rockin' the short hair?"

Garrett grasped her face in his hands and leaned down, giving her a fierce kiss on the lips. "You'll love it, babe. Trust me."

She trusted him with everything she had, so she'd do it one more time. Even if she were unsure about how he would look. "Let's go." She giggled as she grabbed EJ from Shell and strapped him into the stroller.

Hannah and Shell walked ahead of the guys, pushing EJ through the paths of the zoo. He played with toys they'd put in his stroller with him as they made their way from exhibit to exhibit.

"How's it going in the studio?" Shell asked.

Hannah had a lot to fill her in on. Shell had purposely kept her distance, allowing Hannah the freedom to do what she wanted without anyone micromanaging her. It'd been the first time she'd ever been allowed the luxury, and she loved it. "Really great, next week though, I want you to come in and listen to the couple of songs we've finished. I almost have enough for an album, so not too much longer. We're hoping to drop by November."

"Damn, girl." Shell whistled. "That's freaky fast."

"I know." She nodded, looking a little awestruck. "Kurt's listened to me, and he's seen where my vision is going, and he's backing me the whole way. This has been the least stressful situation I've ever been in," she admitted. "So it's moving along a lot quicker. When I don't have to fight for everything I want, stuff happens.

Remember the stress of last time? Garrett out in California, us trying to buy a house? None of that this time. I have my husband, son, and dog to come home to every night, and it's helped me more than I thought it would."

"Well, you just let me know when you want me there, and I'll be there. I've been waiting to take my cue from you, but if you're this close to being done, we need to really work on the marketing package. Next week, give me a few ideas of what you're thinking look-wise, and I'll talk to some stylists for you. Everyone will need to be ready to hit the ground running once everything is mixed."

"Agreed." Hannah nodded. It felt good to have control over where she was going, to have her crap together, for lack of a better word. Maybe that's what had been missing before. She'd let everybody direct her and put her on their time schedules. She'd more than proven this time, if she were left alone with her vision and someone else who believed in it, she could get things done in half the time.

"Babe."

Garrett's voice carried like no one else's, she'd know that *babe* anywhere. She stopped and turned around. "Yeah?"

"We're gonna go get something to drink, you two want anything?"

She and Shell gave him their orders, along with EJ and his diaper bag so he could take care of that as well, and the two of them sat down while they waited for the guys to come back.

"How are things going with Jared?" Hannah asked, glancing over at her friend. Lately, Shell had a glow about her that made Hannah wonder.

"Really good." Shell beamed. Immediately she glanced down at her wedding set, circling it around her ring finger. "Almost too good. It makes me nervous, but I think it'll always be that way."

"Lately you kind of have a glow," Hannah pressed lightly.

Throwing her head back, Shell laughed. "Oh hell no, I've been doing CrossFit with him. As much as I hate to admit it, the endorphins it gives you is incredible." She glanced around. "Don't let him know I told you that. I still like to bitch about it."

She and Shell were still giggling about it when the guys came back with drinks.

"I'm gonna hold him for a little while," Garrett told her. "He was getting hot in that stroller, and I think he needs to burn off some energy."

"If you saw the way he ran from the bathroom to the snack bar, like zero to five thousand, you'd know the energy he has to burn off." Jared shook his head, glancing at the toddler. "I didn't even know he could go that fast."

Hannah grinned up at her son. "Sounds good to me." She consulted the map. "Do you wanna go over to the giraffes and then hit the playground? They have one here for little kids. Maybe he'll be ready to take a nap afterward."

He carried EJ as Jared pushed his stroller, giving them the option of walking as a family. She loved when Garrett held their son, loved the way his biceps bulged slightly, loved the way his big hands encompassed almost their son's entire body. She knew how safe she felt in his arms and loved that EJ felt just as safe. Even now he leaned his head against his dad's shoulder, nibbling on a banana the guys had bought him at the snack counter. He had no cares in the world and had no doubt his dad could protect him from anything.

Her phone dinged in her pocket, and she grabbed it, noticing she had a photo she'd been tagged in on Instagram. Pulling the picture up, she saw it was a picture of them probably taken minutes before, walking.

"People know we're at the zoo. Do you think we should leave, or you think it'll be okay?" she asked as she showed him the picture.

"We'll stay unless a lot of people start to approach us. I think we'll be fine." He put his arm around her neck, pulling her into his body as they walked.

She wanted to melt against him. There wasn't one person who could make her feel safer than her husband. She loved the way he put his arm around her shoulders and hugged her to him. There had never been a place built for her like this; she fit perfectly tucked there, with EJ perched on his other shoulder. If anyone looked at them, they'd see a man who'd once been one of the wildest she'd ever heard of domesticated and happy with his wife and son. Nothing else made her heart fuller and happier than to realize how far Garrett had come. She'd come a long way, but so had he, and together they were making an amazing life for their son and any other kids they might have in the future.

Hannah was thinking about that more often than she had before, which was crazy considering she was back in the studio and getting ready to embark on the craziness of tour life. But she had to admit, seeing her baby boy grow up was making her really want another one. For now though, she'd keep that thought to herself.

Chapter Eleven

"I love this picture." Hannah grinned later on that night as she lay on the couch in Garrett's arms, looking at her phone.

When they'd gotten to the giraffes, EJ had been more excited than they'd imagined and perked right up. Shell had snapped a picture of them as a family, and it had immediately become her new favorite.

"That is a really good one." Garrett yawned as he put his arms around her. "Today was a really good day." He clasped his hands at her waist, resting his chin on her shoulder.

She loved when she sat like this, every inch of her body encompassed by him, his hot breath on her neck, his big hands at her stomach. There wasn't an inch of their bodies that didn't touch each other, and there wasn't a part of her that didn't feel completely wrapped up in his love.

"It was. I'm so glad we can still do stuff like this with him. I worry that at some point maybe we won't be able to." She bit her lip as she scrolled through the pictures on Instagram that people had tagged them in.

"Nah, I think it's fine," Garrett soothed. "As long as people don't start coming up and asking for things, and as long as we teach EJ about strangers, things will be fine. You see all these pictures, but not one damn person bothered us. I think that says a lot about the respect level here in Nashville. I'm not sure we could do that in Huntington Beach." He pushed her hair back from her neck. "I don't regret for one second that we make this our home."

Neither did she, but it was nice to hear him say it every once in a while. "I don't know why I get worried about this stuff randomly."

"You're a mom." He rubbed his chin against her bare shoulder. "He's your son, and you're protective of him. But you know," he dropped his lips to her neck, "that I'm your husband and I'm his dad, and you also know how protective I am of the two of you. They'd have to get through me to get to either one of you, and you know I've got some big shoulders and some rough edges. Nobody will ever take what's mine."

She loved when he went all alpha male. Some women might see it as setting back the feminist movement, but good Lord; he made her hot when he talked like that. "Trust me, I know you'll protect us, I know that with everything I have, but people make me nervous because they're wild cards. We don't know what's going on in their lives. But," she clasped her hand with his, "I won't allow EJ to be scared to go out in public because of who we are, or because of what any of my own hang-ups are."

"See." Garrett kissed her again. "You're a mom, and you want the best for your son. It's okay to have these fears, babe. Just don't let them take over your life."

She breathed deeply as she leaned against him, happy he agreed with her. There had been times they had been scared to go out in public—situations overseas where they'd felt actual fear. Hannah refused to let her child feel that kind of fear.

"Someday there's going to come a time, though. You know that, right?"

"We'll prepare him when that time comes. My wish is he can grow up with as much normalcy as we can give him, until he's ready to embrace the public life." She carefully chose her words.

There was no doubt in her mind their son would follow in his dad's footsteps. The indication was there already. When they watched Black Friday play, EJ would stomp his feet, clap his hands, and she was pretty sure even at the age of one he knew how to headbang with the best of them.

"I don't know why you're worrying about it right now," Garrett commented as he moved his hand up and over the top of the shorts she wore. Feeling his big hand spanning her stomach was one of her favorite things.

"It's kinda what I do." She shrugged. It was the nature of the beast. Being in the public eye for so long caused her to worry about things at the most inopportune times.

Sighing, she went back to her phone, scrolling through the thousands of pictures she had been tagged in. Resting the back of her head against Garrett's chest, she continued to look, clicking on certain tags, smiling or giggling when something caught her eye or struck her as funny. He continued to stroke her stomach, and she thought nothing about it.

Until about five minutes into her scroll, when she felt his hand start moving towards her chest. Immediately, her breath started to come a little faster, and her heart kicked up its beat. Glancing at the clock on the cable box, she saw it was almost midnight. EJ was asleep and would be for hours. Havock was upstairs with him, and for all intents and purposes, she was completely alone with her husband. Waiting to see what he would do, she all but held her breath.

It was a slow trek, but his hand made it all the way up to the edge of her bra. Trying to act like it didn't affect her was becoming harder—much like the appendage poking her from behind. His fingers didn't stop at the band around her chest; they continued up, both hands palming the lacy cups, causing her flesh to overflow, until skin touched skin.

"How about I take your mind off of that little worrying thing you like to do?"

Garrett's voice was deep in her ear; it was the voice she loved. The lazy, sexy, aroused voice that let her know in no uncertain terms she was in for a good time. If anyone had ever told her she'd be the type of person to enjoy such a physical relationship with her husband, she would have said they were lying.

But here she was. Nipples hard. Heart pounding.

Panties wet. And he'd just taken her to heaven the night before.

Hannah laid her head back against his shoulder and sighed as she closed her eyes. The sigh was the sound of her giving in to whatever her husband wanted to do to her.

"Relax," he whispered in her ear as one hand smoothly made its way down her stomach, slipping into the waistband of the shorts she wore. The fingers pushed past the edges of the panties covering the hot spot of her body that wanted him the most. As soon as he made contact, she groaned deeply, pushing up against him.

"I got you, Han." His voice was deep, a growl, not the soothing tone he normally used with her.

His other hand pushed the lacy cup of the bra she wore down in a quick motion, leaving her skin bare to his palm. Roughly he cupped it, pushing his flesh against hers, grasping until he held the hard nub of her nipple between his forefinger and thumb.

"Garrett," she breathed as he went back and forth between her two breasts. He pulled in time with his finger strumming what had become a super sensitive clit.

"You're so wet," he spoke in her ear. His voice deep, dark; his tone the sexiest she'd ever heard.

Her eyes closed, she let herself be overtaken by her other senses. Her sense of touch, her sense of sound. Hannah rotated her hips towards his fingers, using her feet and legs to push closer to the fingers wreaking havoc on her body.

"So warm, so tight," he was still saying in her ear.

"Always so goddamn ready for me." His own breath stuttered, and it caused her nipples to tighten even harder.

She reached behind her, grabbing his thighs, using the leverage to push up against his hand, to take his fingers deeper as they plunged into her warmth. Breathing heavily through her nose, she let out a whine as he crushed his palm against her clit, giving her the contact she needed.

"My dick's so hard." Garrett continued weaving his spell around her. "As soon as you come, I'm taking what's mine. So good," he breathed heavily in her ear, reaching out with his tongue to caress the lobe before he lightly grazed it with his teeth. "Gonna feel so good as I fuck you with aftershocks still coursing through your body from this orgasm I'm about to give you. Won't even take my sweatpants off, just gonna push 'em down until I can get my cock out, gonna rip your shorts and panties off, and then I'm gonna get mine. You want that don't you, babe?"

God, yes, she wanted it. She wanted it more than she wanted the orgasm she could feel approaching at lightning speed. "Yes," she answered. "I want it so bad."

"Then take it." He picked up the pace with his fingers. "Take it, baby. Get there."

Hannah did as she was told, taking her pleasure, turning her head so she could grab his lips with hers, using his mouth to quieten her cries of pleasure.

True to his word, before she realized what was going on, he'd flipped them over so she lay on the couch, panties gone, shorts gone, and his body over the top of hers. As she looked down, his hand steadying his cock as he drove it home, she pushed her head back against the arm of the couch, ready to let him take her wherever he wanted her to go.

Chapter Twelve

Garrett couldn't believe how hot she'd made him, just by being Hannah. He'd been almost positive when they'd gotten married that at some point sex would become just sex—it happened to almost every couple—but he'd been surprised every time they'd come together like this. Sometimes it was sweet, slow, and passionate; other times it was hot, dirty, and completely out-of-this-world exciting. He loved that he was the man who'd helped her discover this side of herself. Loved even more that he was the only man who'd ever get to see her lose herself the way she did with him.

"Every time with you, it's like I feel something new," he rasped into her ear as he braced himself by grasping the arm of the couch with both hands.

His arms encircled her face, and he used the opportunity to bend down and capture her lips with his. It was a slow but intense fuck this time. He wouldn't pull all the way out, but he let himself go deep, grinding against her mound, drinking in the soft sounds she made.

The coupling was powerful; made even more so

when she reached up, lacing her fingers through his. The connection he had with her was one he'd never had with another person before, and sometimes it threatened to smother him. Right when he felt like he couldn't breathe, a huge gasp of air would flow through his lungs, and he'd realize how much he loved her, and it all felt brand new again. He'd never had that before, and knew he'd never need to have it again. Just the thought of not having Hannah in his life caused him to squeeze their entwined fingers as he thrust again, this time slower, but harder and deeper, causing them both to shiver.

Their shirts rubbed against each other, creating friction, making his chest warm. A trickle of sweat worked its way down his back. He was so attuned to everything going on around them, happening to them, he could feel the moisture as it made its journey. It added to the eroticism of the encounter, but it wasn't until Hannah let go of his fingers to take his shirt in both her fists that he picked up the pace.

She stretched the fabric taut against his body, using it to help her move against him. Finally, they came up for air, gasping, panting, and hot for each other. Taking one hand off the couch, he moved it down her side, exposing the tattoo on her hip bone, rubbing the ink with his thumb.

"I got you; you know I got you," he encouraged her, dipping his head to her collar bone, sucking, biting, nipping, as she went wild beneath him. At his spine, he felt her hands move to his ass, gripping the naked skin under the fleece of his sweatpants, digging her nails in as she thrust, grunted, and groaned with him.

When the climax came, it came for both of them. He glanced up from his spot at her collarbone, seeing her mouth open in a silent "O", watching her head fall back, and that was all it took for Garrett to feel the hot rush of completion as he sucked her skin.

As they lay together minutes later, hearts pounding, wiping away sweat from each other's skin, he wondered, like he always did, how many more times she could blow his mind.

It had been a struggle for Hannah to get out of bed this Monday morning, especially after the weekend she'd had with her family. But she'd gotten through it, calling Shell on her way in, asking her to meet so they could start going over some preliminary marketing strategies. She and Kurt only had three more songs to finish, and then they would be turning the album in.

"You don't think that strays away too far from how people know me?" she asked Kurt as they finished listening to a number that was way more reminiscent of Miranda Lambert than Harmony Stewart.

Kurt shook his head as he turned off the track. "Listeners are definitely going to take into account who you're married to. I mean you share a lot of your life on social media; they know exactly who your husband is and the type of music he plays. It only makes sense some of his style rub off on you, and I think that's what this is. Do I think it's going to be played on rock radio? No.

This is still very much in-line with you and who you are. It's not like you've completely changed. You're just growing and evolving. Thank you for letting me be a part of it."

She smiled brightly at his words. He got it. Everything she'd wanted to do with this record, he'd supported her. Now she hoped the record company got it too.

"So we have these three left to finish?" She pointed out the three names on the whiteboard they'd been using.

"That's it, and then you're done, Ms. Hannah. We'll turn it into the record label and see what they say."

Her next words she'd mulled over in her head a lot, and when she spoke them aloud, she meant them with everything she had. "I don't care what they say. I'm really proud of it."

"I am too." He gave her a high-five. "So let's get in there and get these done. Shell's supposed to be here today, right?"

"She'll be here in a few hours to go over the things we need to do to get the marketing campaign going."

He turned around in his chair and pointed at the booth. "Let's go ahead and get this work out of the way so you can concentrate on what she'll want you to do when she gets here." He stopped her before she fully closed the door. "Hannah."

"Yeah?" She'd never heard the tone in his voice before, the urgency that made her turn around without pause.

"This album is going to blow you into the stratosphere. Don't forget where you come from, your family, your friends, your convictions, and don't forget the love your husband has for you. It's all over every single one of these songs. It's inevitable you'll find yourself struggling to stay grounded after all is said and done. When you're swooped up by not only the Nashville machine but the world, remember who you are right at this moment, and don't let anybody push you to be someone you're not."

"I won't," she said, and she meant it with every single fiber of her being.

Hannah bit her nails as she watched Shell's expressions. For ten songs she'd sat without saying a word, making notes of things here and there on a piece of paper in front of her. Now they were at the end, and Hannah was positively vibrating with excitement, wanting to beg and plead with her friend to tell her what she thought. When the last chords of the song faded out, she couldn't wait any longer.

"Well? What did you think?"

Shell was quiet for a few seconds, the longest seconds of Hannah's life. A small grin broke across her face that turned into a huge smile. "I love it! I mean fucking love it! It's so much different than your old stuff, but in the same vein too. I don't know how to explain it. It's everything we've loved about Harmony Stewart for years, but it's edgier, rockier, and just plain better than anything you've ever put out before."

"I'm so relieved." Hannah put a hand to her heart, trying to slow the pounding. The longer Shell hadn't said anything, the more nervous she'd gotten. "So what are your ideas?"

"Oh girl, I have pages." She held up the notes she'd been taking throughout the first listen. "I'm gonna type all this up for you with some bullet points that I think are going to make or break this campaign, and I'll get it emailed to you. When do you deliver the record?"

"I'm sending it tonight." She wrung her hands in a nervous gesture. "I'm not sure how they're going to react. It's different."

Shell grinned as she got up and walked over to her friend, hugging her fiercely. "Do you remember when we first met Garrett and the guys? We kept saying how different they were, but then we realized different didn't always mean worse?"

"I distinctly remember when that happened."

"Well, I'm telling you this right here, right now." She let go and pointed at Kurt. "What the two of you have done here is nothing short of amazing, and you don't know how badly I want to tease the fans with some of the songs I heard tonight. But I'll be good. I'll wait until the record label hears it, until they give me the green light. Damn, this is going to be huge though. Mark my words. The world's not going to know what hit them."

Hannah smiled as she celebrated with her friends. With the touch of a button she sent the album to the record label and to Garrett. She still trusted his opinion above everyone else's. But deep down, she was worried. Part of her was worried this album would tank, the other part was worried it'd do as well as everyone seemed to think it would. She was in a hell of a spot right now. Wanting to be a performer, wanting to be a mom, and wanting to be a wife.

One thing was for sure. She'd be getting a crash course in how to be all three soon and hopefully with a successful album to boot.

She grabbed her cell phone as she saw a FaceTime request coming from Garrett. Answering, she grinned. "Wow, that was quick. I *just* sent you the album."

"Unfortunately, that's not why I'm calling." He directed the phone behind him where EJ was running a million miles an hour. "Someone doesn't want to lie down for a nap. Remember when I told you I needed your secrets? Now would be good."

"Grab the phone and lie down with him on the couch, even if he fights you about it. Make sure he can see me on the screen."

Garrett did as he was told, fighting with their son the entire way. When EJ saw Hannah's face on the screen, he calmed down, glancing at her.

"You ready to go to sleep, EJ?" she asked in a soothing voice.

He shook his head *no*, and she patiently began to sing. To everyone who watched, it was obvious they'd been through this once or twice. She sang softly to him, two songs, before his eyes started to droop, and then on the third, he was out like a light.

"There you go," she whispered to Garrett, who was looking sleepy himself.

"Thanks, babe. I'll listen to the album when we wake up."

She laughed. "Enjoy your nap."

What she wouldn't give to be enjoying nap time with the both of them right now.

Chapter Thirteen

"Yes sir, I totally agree."

Hannah sat in her kitchen along with EJ, Shell, Garrett, Jared, and Havock as they listened to the conversation Shell was having with the head of the record label. Things seemed to be going in her favor, but she wouldn't know for sure until Shell finished the phone call. She watched as Shell frantically made notes. For a while Hannah had tried to read them, but Shell had her own version of shorthand that only she could understand.

"Do you think they like it?" She leaned over as she quietly talked to Garrett.

"I have absolutely no idea, but I can tell you I loved it." He slung his arm around her neck, pulling her in close enough so he could drop a kiss on her forehead. "For real though, I can't wait to see what kind of tight leather pants you rock on some of the heavier numbers. You'll try those on for me, right?"

She blushed as she turned her head into his shoulder. "You know you always get your own private show."

The group went back to listening to Shell's end of the conversation. She'd been on the phone with the head of the record label's PR and a few other VIPs for over an hour. Hannah wasn't sure if that was good or bad. She tried to never really be privy to this information, because it made her so nervous, but this season in her life was different than any other situation they'd been in before.

Glancing to the end of the counter, she saw EJ in his high chair, playing intently with the Play Dough Jared and Shell had brought him. Jared was turning a blob of orange into something that was making EJ laugh, and she couldn't help but think about how good of a dad Jared would be when they decided to have kids.

"I don't know how much longer I can take this," she whispered to Garrett. "I just need a thumbs up or something."

"You wanna go outside?" he asked, turning to face her.

Why not, she was doing nothing right now other than imagining the worst. "Do you want to take EJ?"

"Nah." He pointed over to EJ and Jared. "They're having fun together."

"When she gets off the phone, will you have her come find me?" Hannah told Jared as she and Garrett made their way outside.

It was a crisp morning, with the smell of fall in the air and some of the lingering heat of the summer still pounding down from the sky. Highs had dropped into the seventies, and over-night they were bottoming out into the fifties. This was her favorite kind of weather.

Soon Halloween would be upon them, along with bonfires, s'mores, sweaters, and boots. She wondered where she would be then. Would they immediately make her start touring? Would she get to enjoy those first few days of fall with her family? Would she be able to take him trick or treating? Everything was up in the air now, and she hated feeling like she had no place to land.

"C'mon." Garrett grabbed her hand, pulling her to the back of their property. There he'd set up some playground equipment he and Jared used to work out on. There was a pull-up bar, and she knew he normally liked to do pullups with weights, but she didn't see any around today. Taking his shirt off, he threw it at her in a playful manner, grinning when she wolf-whistled for him.

She watched as he went over to the bar and stood beneath it. "I need weight, come hang out with me." He motioned for her.

She'd done this a few times, and she had to admit it was one of the hottest things he'd ever asked her to do. He bent down so she could loop her arms around his neck, hanging on as he hopped up, getting a tight grip on the bar. As he started lifting them up and down, he spoke.

"Tell me what's got you so messed up."

The same question had been mulling around in her own head. She wasn't sure why she was so nervous. There had been many times in her career when the record label had hated what she'd done. They'd decided the direction she was going in wasn't one she should be going in. It had never really bothered her before, probably because for the most part she'd given in to them. With this album, she didn't want to give in; she didn't want them to decide for her what was going to happen. She'd put a piece of herself and, if she were being honest, a piece of Reaper into this record too. He encouraged her to think outside the box, do things she wouldn't normally be comfortable with doing, and flash a middle finger to the establishment. While that wasn't normally her style, she'd done just that with this record, and if someone threatened it, if they questioned her authority to do what she wanted, she wasn't sure how she'd deal with it.

"What if they hate it?"

"So what if they do, Han? It won't be the first time, won't be the last time, and really does it matter? You're happy with it."

"But it does matter," she argued. "Kurt's the only person who ever asks for my opinion in the studio. He took *my* direction. What if they hate it and it reflects badly on him? I don't want to be known as the trouble child of Music Row."

He chuckled as he continued lifting the two of them up and down. "I'm not sure anyone could ever label you as a trouble child, but think whatever you want. I personally think you've given them something different, something they didn't expect, and I think they're trying to figure out how to market it and you at the same time. You're different now, just like you were different after we first started dating. It took a while, but eventually everyone came on board with it."

He was right. She needed to woman up and realize things would always be a fight, but in the end, everyone wanted to make money, and she knew without a doubt this record would make the money the record label wanted. As she opened her mouth to speak, she saw the back door open, and out poured Shell, Jared, EJ, and Havock.

"I guess they have an answer," he said as he dropped down from his bar. The impact with the ground jarred her, but she let go and steadied herself. "Let's go see what that answer is. Are you ready?"

As ready as she'd ever be.

"Just give it to me straight," she told Shell as they all met in the middle of the yard.

"They love it." Shell's voice was excited, tremoring with the possibility of all the cool things she knew were coming. "The first TV spots will drop the first week of November, and the album will be scheduled for a Thanksgiving release."

"Are you kidding me?" she questioned, unable to believe this was her life. Big time artists dropped right before Christmas.

"They're working on the press junket now, but let me just say enjoy the next week and a half here at home, because we'll be hitting radio, talk shows, and everything known to man after that. Since this isn't exactly a straight-up country record, they're pushing you for pop radio too, Han. This could be huge."

Hannah almost had to sit down. To crossover was something she'd never really considered, and to know the record company was going to attempt it was a big step in their faith of her. "They agreed to everything?"

"Including bringing your family on the road and concerts no more than three nights in a row. They believe in this Han, they believe in you. What it looks like now is they want this to be a huge tour, depending on how the first single drops. Multiple nights in big markets." Shell couldn't keep the smile off her face. "You did it, you did what you wanted to do, and I think they realize what they have in this record. You sound mature, your voice is better than it's ever been, and the public wants you. They miss you, and you've picked the perfect time to come back."

Garrett grabbed her around the waist. "Are you ready for this?"

Was she ready? It was a question she'd been asking herself all day. How would she juggle this? How would she make sure everyone had what they needed, including herself? "As long as I have all of you by my side, I can do anything."

Garrett picked her up and swung her around, his smile infectious. "Then let's take over the world, babe, one radio market at a time."

With him smiling at her—she had all the confidence in the world she could.

Chapter Fourteen

"I hope it doesn't rain." Hannah bit her lip in apprehension as their little family hit the interstate, heading out of Nashville to a private farm in Franklin.

The record company had taken her suggestion and were letting her do the album photography the way she wanted. She wanted all of them on the cover, and they'd been good with it.

"If it does, they have that huge barn," Garrett mumbled as he checked his blind spot, accelerating onto the interstate.

He was right; they'd been there before when a mutual friend had gotten married. It was beautiful and everything she wanted for the photo shoot, but she still hoped it wouldn't rain.

"Are you sure you're okay with being on the cover?"

Garrett chuckled. "Yeah, babe, I think I'm man enough to take it."

"Oh, I have no doubt you're man enough to take it, but I worry you might be made fun of."

He cut a glance in her direction. "I have the hottest

wife ever, and I get to have a seriously fun photo shoot with my family. If people make fun of it they're fuckin' assholes."

She sat back against her seat, knowing he was telling the truth. She still worried, like she always did, if he'd regret marrying her and not someone who was more like him.

"It's this turn off isn't it?" he pointed to a gated drive.

"Yeah, let me grab the gate code." She reached over into her purse, grabbing her phone.

They got in with no problem, and he kept driving until they saw some cars, a trailer, and a couple of people milling around. "I asked them to keep it low-key." She grinned. "I wasn't sure how EJ would handle it—or Havock."

When she said the dog's name, his ears perked up.

"Yeah, boy, you're a part of the family, aren't you," Garrett playfully spoke to him.

Havock barked loudly, causing everybody to laugh.

They exited the car, Garrett holding EJ so he wouldn't run off, Havock's leash in his hand. "Alright, babe, go see what you need to do, and we'll be here waiting. I promise he won't get dirty."

She'd worked with the photographer a couple of times and was very comfortable with her. They'd gone to high school together.

"Hey, Laura." She waved as she made her way over to the set-up.

"Hey, girl, it's so good to see you! Thanks for putting

my name down for this," she greeted her with a hug.

"No problem. I knew I wanted it done here, and I love your eye. Mom showed me the pictures you took of her and dad last year. They were fantastic, and that's something like what I want here."

"I'm assuming you want a few for your own collection too?" Laura asked, trying to get a feel of what she would be doing today.

"Definitely. The only thing I ask with the album pictures is that you don't show EJ's face, I know I do on my Instagram and stuff, but I feel like putting his face out there like *that* would be asking for trouble," she explained, hoping she wouldn't make her friend mad.

"Totally understandable." She made notes on a piece of paper beside her. "And you want your dog in the pictures too, right?"

She grinned. "He's a part of the family."

"Aren't they always?" Laura gave a wry grin as she flashed her phone to Hannah. There she saw a picture of a beautiful dog and cat. "Those are mine and they rule the roost. I have one more question. Album title. I need to know how much blank space I leave in the frame."

"It's called *I Got You.* Pretty short, but personal to me." She thought back to the tattoo she now sported.

"Alright, I'm ready to go when you are. I'm assuming you don't need makeup, looks like you've already taken care of that yourself."

"No, I'm good."

"Okay, then let's get the show on the road."

It was hours before they were done, but all of them agreed they were fun hours. There were a lot of laughs, a couple of tears from EJ, and a ton of smiles as the day was captured on film.

"I want you two to come over here and look at this one. Hannah, I think this one will probably be the album cover." Laura waved them over to where she'd downloaded the pictures onto her computer.

"Oh wow," Garrett breathed as he saw it. Their backs were to the camera. He stood next to Hannah with his arm around her waist, to her other side EJ stood, holding her hand, and Havock sat patiently next to EJ who had his arm around the dog.

"I think it kind of cements the whole album title." She smiled. "They totally are holding you up in this picture."

"They are," Hannah agreed, doing her best to keep the emotions out of her voice.

"And, I have the front version too." She switched to another picture on the computer.

"Oh my gosh, I love it." Hannah beamed as she saw the front. "Can we have that one?"

"Yeah, let me text it over to you right now. I have some others that I got, and some you don't know that I got. I'll send them all over to you in the next few days," she promised.

Hannah quickly texted the same picture to Garrett, as they packed up, getting ready to leave.

"Thanks again for letting me do this." Laura shook hands with Garrett. "And it's really nice to meet you. You're just as nice as everyone said you were."

Garrett hitched EJ up higher on his hip. The little boy had fallen into a deep sleep not more than fifteen minutes before. "I've mellowed out with age. Just be glad you met me now and not ten years ago."

"Don't we all mellow with age?"

Hannah winked. "I'll keep all your secrets, Laura, don't worry."

Just as they got into their SUV and Garrett started it up, the sky opened and rain came pouring down. Hannah couldn't help but laugh. "Well at least it waited until we were done."

"I don't know." Garrett looked over at her. "I would have kinda liked it."

Hannah glanced around. Laura and her crew were already driving away; Havock and EJ were both asleep. "I'm game if you are. Leave the car running for them." She quirked a brow.

Unbuckling her seat belt, she opened the door and bolted out into the rain. It was still warm in the south, so neither one of them had to be worried about being cold. Garrett came around the SUV, glasses off, running towards her.

"Sometimes you surprise the hell outta me." He grabbed her hands and they twirled round and round before he pulled her into his arms.

"Sometimes I surprise myself."

She reached up, kissing him full and hard on the mouth, enjoying the moment alone they were having together. It was weird, but every once in a while, in the middle of her crazy life, she had moments like this that completely took her breath away.

Chapter Fifteen

"What time is it supposed to run?" Garrett asked.

He and Hannah sat on their couch in their living room. It was a normal Wednesday night, or it had been until they'd gotten a phone call from her record label an hour ago. They'd informed her they would be running a spot on a very popular reality singing competition, teasing the public of her upcoming album. They would also be releasing the video she'd recorded a week before for the debut single at midnight on her VeVo channel. To say they were both nervous was the understatement of the year.

"Halfway in," she answered, a dazed expression on her face. "They said they want to make sure people are in invested and paying attention when the spot drops."

"Are you okay?" He felt like it was a valid question. She hadn't been involved in the whirlwind of promoting an album, having new music out, or even having the expectation in a long time. His worst fear was she would become completely consumed and fall back into bad habits.

She glanced at him, her dark eyes cloudy with emotions he couldn't translate. For years she'd been an open book to him, he'd been able to tell with one look how she felt, and now it seemed she was possibly closing herself off to him. "Don't do it, Han. Let's talk this out."

"I'm scared," she whispered. "I know I said I was doing this because I was bored, and I wanted something to do because EJ didn't need me as much anymore, but now I'm scared nobody is excited about it." She tilted her head back against the couch, closing her eyes as she continued speaking. "Somewhere in the middle of all this, it became a journey for me. One I believe wholeheartedly in. We made an amazing album, and if people don't love it, I'm afraid it'll break me. I realized somewhere along the line, I *do* need to be Harmony Stewart. It's not that being your wife and being his mom isn't enough for me, but I need an identity of my own. Garrett, what if I messed around and lost that?"

"You didn't," he assured her, taking her into his arms. "There is so much buzz and excitement about this already. You just can't see it; you're too focused on the negative. Babe, people have missed you. This will blow up. I don't know how else to make you believe."

Snuggling next to him, she pulled her bottom lip in between her teeth. "I guess that's really it. I'm not going to believe it until I see it, and I'm not going to see it until it's out there for the public to consume. It's a catch-22. I'm so scared," she admitted. "I put a lot of myself into this record, more than I thought I would. I ended up writing all but two of the songs, and if people don't love what I've done, it's gonna break my heart."

"And if that happens, I'll be there to put it back together. But things are going to be fine," he soothed her, kissing her on the forehead.

"This is it." She grabbed his hand as they played two lines of the lead single from her new album against a black screen. Then four words appeared, and she felt goosebumps rise on every party of her body.

"I'm back—Harmony Stewart"

She really felt as if she was, especially with the excitement fluttering in her stomach. This kind of excitement hadn't been there since her newly signed days. The tension in the room was palpable.

"That like twenty seconds of TV was the most suspenseful twenty seconds I've ever experienced." Garrett laughed as he pulled her hand up to his lips, kissing her lightly.

"I know." She breathed deeply. "I just don't even know what to think about any of it."

"Where's your phone?" he asked, glancing around for it.

"Charging. It died earlier." She wasn't sure why he all of a sudden wanted her phone. Normally when they spent time together in the evenings like this, all phones were put away. This was their time, no one else was normally allowed.

"Go get it." He pushed her off the couch. "I bet you have a ton of notifications."

It dawned on her what he was saying, but something stopped her. She sat back down on the couch, frozen by something she hadn't felt in a very long time. Fear. The fear of failure. "But what if I don't? What if I missed my shot?"

"You didn't miss your shot."

She shot him a glance. "You don't know that."

"And neither do you, unless you go get the goddamn phone, Hannah. Stop psyching yourself out."

His tone was harsh, one he hadn't used with her in a long time, but she needed it. If she couldn't be strong enough for herself, she would need him to pick up the slack, to help her stand tall; otherwise she would fall under the weight. It would cripple her like a column in an earthquake, and she knew this time she couldn't allow that to happen. Not like she had in the past. She was a mother now, a wife, and a businesswoman—one who had her own place in the world and who knew her worth. It was time she acted like it.

"Go get the phone." He pointed to the counter where it always charged.

Getting up, she locked her legs, not allowing him to see she was shaking. It was horrible being vulnerable and putting her insecurities out there for anyone to see, but this was her husband. He'd understand more than anyone else. He'd been there through the worst of them all. She slowed down as she got to the phone. But what if there were *no* notifications? What if nobody gave a crap anymore? What would be worse? A ton or none? The bad thing about it...she wasn't sure.

Stop, Hannah! She hadn't been this neurotic in a long time. *Grab the phone and look at the screen. Just like pulling a bandage off a wound.*

Leaning forward, she grabbed her phone, turned off the lock screen, and ripped that bandage off.

"Garrett," she breathed, a shocked note that even she heard in her voice.

"Babe, you okay?" He got up and walked over to where she stood, the phone in her hand. Looking over her shoulder, he did a double take as he saw her notification numbers. "Holy fucking shit." They were bordering on the five digit marks, and the teaser had played less than five minutes ago.

"I'm scared but excited. I want to see what people have said, but I'm nervous they think it was crap." The nervousness in her voice jumbled all the words together. Her hands shook as she extended the phone out to him. "You look, and please let me down easy if it's bad."

Grabbing the phone, he opened up her apps, doing a quick scroll of what he could see. A giant smile forming on his face. "Babe, people are so fucking excited. You have to read these." He grabbed her hand and pulled her so that her back was to his front.

Being this close to him was good for her. She could project all her fears onto him, he would absorb them, and it would leave her with a peace she hadn't had before.

"Really?" She opened her eyes and watched as his finger scrolled the comments on her phone. He was telling the truth. There were so many exclamation points it was making her head spin. "Oh my God, Garrett, they loved what they heard!"

The magnitude finally dawned on her as she turned around and jumped into his arms, wrapping her legs around his waist.

"They did, baby." He chuckled. "They did."

"I'm so relieved," she admitted as she buried her face in his neck. "Country is so different. When you leave for a while, there's no guarantee people will love you when you come back. I was truly scared they wouldn't accept me because so many people felt like I turned on them when I decided to stay home. To know they want me back…" She stopped, emotion strangling her voice and tears spilling over her cheeks. For the first time, she felt accepted, wanted, and missed by people who sometimes had made her feel less than good about herself. It was a moment she'd never forget. Clinging to Garrett's neck, she sobbed—for the girl who'd always thought nobody had really cared, and for the woman who'd been shown an amazing amount of love and adoration. In becoming a wife and a mother, she'd become relatable to everyone, and they showed her how much by welcoming her back when they didn't have to.

"Are you ready?" he asked the question in a low voice, truly asking her if she was ready for all this.

The moment held a palpable tension, and they both knew they were on the precipice of something bigger than the both of them. This *would* change their lives.

"I'm ready."

Chapter Sixteen

Her dining and living room area had been turned into the biggest dressing room Hannah had ever seen. Garrett and EJ sat in the floor coloring, Havock slept in the corner, and in the middle of it all, she and Shell were working with a stylist. They'd tried on no less than five hundred outfits, she was sure.

"What about the sundress?" Cameron, the stylist for the day, asked as she rummaged through the racks she'd hung up.

Hannah thought it over. The sundress was cute, and she'd probably wear it in her day-to-day life, but Harmony was ready for a change. She was ready to get on stage and kick some…well, you know. "I think I want to go with edgier pieces this time. I don't want people to see me as they've always seen me. I've changed."

"She's got a hot husband and a super cute son now," Garrett spoke up from where he sat on the floor, EJ in his lap.

"We're going to make the hot husband go take his equally hot best friend to lunch if he doesn't shut the fuck up." Shell pointed a finger at Garrett, threatening him.

"Hey!" both he and Hannah scolded her as he put his hands over EJ's ears.

"You have to watch it with him now," Garrett told her. "Yesterday, he had a hard time getting his pants on…out of nowhere, he said, 'fuck it'. Like knew how to use the word and everything. Hannah was horrified." He laughed.

Hannah turned to all of them, her face red. "My son," she stopped to take a breath, "can't even speak full sentences yet, but he knows how to correctly use the F-word. I blame all of you, because he didn't get it from me. I'm praying for him, to be honest with you."

They laughed at her indignation.

"See? This is the problem! Y'all need Jesus."

Shell rolled her eyes and spoke to Cameron. "Maybe we can do the leather pants and that tank top? What do you think about that, Han?"

"I still think you need Jesus, but I'm gonna go try the outfit on because it looks cute."

"We're gonna head out, babe." Garrett stood, holding EJ. "Jared just texted and he wants lunch, so we're gonna have a dude day if that's cool with you."

She felt like they always had dude days, but it would probably be easier for her to get what she needed to done without the two of them there. "Have fun, guys." She leaned in, kissing both of them.

"Bye!" EJ waved as he snuggled into his dad's shoulder.

She watched them go, envious of where their son sat. "Okay, ladies." She gave the other two a pointed look. "Let's get this show on the road. When they come back, I wanna spend time with my guys."

Without any added distraction, the three of them got to work, and over the course of the afternoon picked out a whole new wardrobe for her. New hair and makeup would come tomorrow, and then she'd be ready to face the world.

"I'm surprised you decided to come out, with the girls all over at the house," Jared said as he pulled up a kid's booster seat for EJ and the three of them got situated to have lunch together.

Garrett sighed. "Normally it's not that bad, but I hate the way Hannah second guesses herself sometimes, and then when she says what she really means or wants, the stylist is like 'Are you sure?' Then Shell has to speak up and reiterate what Hannah's already said. Dude, it takes everything I have not want to fuck people up who are supposedly there to help Hannah. I don't know why, but they never take her word for it. Never have, if I remember correctly. I can't understand why they feel the need to question her. Hannah's not dumb, and she speaks very highly. As in, she knows what she wants for the most part. It confuses me why they continually question her. They act like she's a little kid who doesn't know her own mind."

Jared thoughtfully chewed and took the time to swallow before he spoke. "I don't want you to be pissed at me when I say this."

"Dude, we're friends."

He laughed. "We are friends. The best of friends, but that doesn't mean I can be totally transparent and honest when it comes to your wife. Which I completely understand. I find myself crazily protective of Shell, especially since I put a ring on her finger. We're just kinda alpha like that."

"Please, give me your advice."

"It's because Hannah's allowed it for so long. *She* looks to Shell for affirmation anytime they're in the same room and Hannah doesn't know the answer. Why wouldn't other people do the same? I'm not saying it's a bad thing. Shell knows her shit, and she's really damn good at her job. But if Hannah deflects to her, why wouldn't everyone else?"

"I get it." Garrett took a drink of his water before he leaned over to help EJ eat his cheese quesadilla. "Trust me when I say I get it, but I didn't actually think it would be so hard for her to take control of her own life. I mean I'd heard things before, but seeing this up close and personal is something else. I'd be so pissed if someone was deflecting to another person about my life, but Hannah just deals."

"Because that's what she's always done and what's she always been expected to do. For people like us," Jared reminded him, "we feel better when other people take over and make decisions for us. Then if it's the wrong decision we can blame others. It's not something we mean to do, or even realize we're doing in the moment, but that's the end result. I think Hannah will start to stand up more for herself, but it's hard, Garrett. It really is, and she's come a long way in a short amount of time. You have to be patient with her and trust that she knows when to stop the madness."

"That's it though. My biggest fear, man," Garrett confessed. "She'll just keep saying yes at the expense of herself, us, and anyone else who needs her to say yes. What happens if she goes back to what she was doing before, what happens if I can't save her?"

"That's a conversation you and she need to have together. I know this because Shell and I have the same conversation at least once every three months or so. It's frustrating for me, but I understand where she's coming from because I know how I am. I don't realize I'm off the rails until I'm completely off, and the only hope of getting me back is putting my ass in rehab again. I don't want to be there, and I know Hannah doesn't either."

Jared watched as Garrett struggled. He didn't know what his friend struggled with, but he wanted to be patient enough to let Garrett work this out on his own. He didn't know what it was like to love someone with an addiction, only knew what it was like to be the person with the addiction. While Hannah had successfully had control over hers for a long time, Jared knew the touring cycle, the scrutiny of the public eye, and the insane amount of pressure she would be under would make it easy for her to slip back into old habits. It was the easiest thing to do when things became too hard or too stressful.

"You have to talk to her; you have to voice your fears to her. She has insecurities like we all do, and chances are she's already thinking what you are."

"My fear…" Garrett's voice was strangled with emotion. It was a tone he didn't readily let people hear, but all his barriers were down with his best friend. "My fear is she'll clam up, tell me I'm dumb, and feel like I'm throwing accusations at her. I'm not and I never would unless I thought something was truly going on. I just want her to know I'm here for her if things start to be too much."

"That's all you gotta tell her, man. Just be upfront, honest, and loving. That's all we want, and I'm telling you that's all she needs. Hannah's smart and she's been where she is right now before. She'll know what she needs from you. Will she ask for it? That's a different question altogether. So why don't you take the question out of it and just let her know you're there no matter what."

Garrett glanced over at his son, the other most important person in his life. "I will. If it makes her mad, then so be it. I'll take her anger any day. But if it saves her hurt, I'll be glad I did."

Chapter Seventeen

G arrett was nervous. After his lunch with Jared, he'd come to the conclusion he needed to talk to Hannah. He needed to see where her head was and make sure there weren't any thoughts hanging around that could be detrimental to her and her ongoing recovery. A conversation like this hadn't happened in over a year— not since she'd lost the baby weight from EJ's pregnancy.

She'd gone to tuck EJ in, and then they had the night to themselves. He'd gotten her a glass of wine and turned the lights down low in the living room. He hoped she would be relaxed and not feel as if he were accusing her of something. That was his biggest fear. He didn't want her to think he didn't trust her.

"He's down," she said as she came into the living room. "Havock stayed up there with him like normal." She laughed softly as she had a seat next to him on their huge couch.

She leaned her head back against the couch and breathed a deep sigh. "I'm tired. Today was a long day."

"Did you finally get the stylist to listen to what you want to wear?" He tried to keep the irritation out of his voice, but it was hard to temper his response.

"Is that why you left?" She glanced over at him.

"I hate when people don't take you or what you say seriously. You know it pisses me off. I hate when they constantly deflect to Shell."

She shrugged. "It's how it's always been. You heard me though; I told her what I wanted, and we had no problems after that. It was a good day," she admitted. "Just tiring. I forgot how much energy all of the things that encompass a tour take."

He was quiet, biting his tongue. He wanted to lay everything out for her but was scared to. It was unlike him to hold back with her, but bringing it up right now felt like he was forcing her hand, much like all those other people did.

"I can tell you want to ask me something, Garrett. Why don't you do it?"

He turned so they were facing one another. It struck him how young she looked right now. No makeup, hair up off her face, wearing one of his T-shirts and a pair of yoga pants. She still looked like a teenager, not the woman who turned him inside out, not the mother of his child, and maybe that was the problem. He'd always want to protect her, because it always seemed like she needed it.

"How are you doing? Do you feel like the pressure is getting to you?"

She leaned over, cupping his face with her hands. "I

love you." She leaned into him, kissing him on the lips.

"I love you too, but I seriously want an answer, Han."

"I'm fine, I promise you." She grabbed his hand. "If I feel like things are about to go out of control, I'll tell you. I have no desire to go back down the road I've already been on. I'm truly in a good place right now, Garrett."

He blew out a deep breath. "Okay, I'll trust you and believe you unless it seems like I can't anymore."

"I know my past and I know where I came from. I know it's hard for you to believe I will be honest with you, because you're used to dealing with Jared, and I'm not going to get angry with you. It'd be easy for me to, because the old me would be offended that you're even asking me this question. This me now knows you do it because you're worried and you love me. I will tell you and ask for help if I need it. I have more than myself to think about now, and I would never ever put our family at risk."

He felt the anxiety release in his chest, felt his breath come easier. Reaching for her, he pulled her into his body, holding her tight. "Things are going to get insane if the internet is any indication. Fans have been waiting on you to come back for a long time. They're foaming at the mouth over your little twenty-second clip. It might pull us apart more than we like."

She grasped his hand, entwining their fingers together. Lifting them up, her voice was strong. "But nobody's gonna break up what's stronger when it's wrapped together, and I am totally wrapped up in you. You hold me up, I'll hold you up?"

"No need to even ask, babe." He kissed her forehead. "I got you."

"When are they loading it?" Hannah asked Shell as they sat at the dining room table.

Friends and family had gathered for a cookout. The first week of November was unseasonably warm in the Nashville area, so they were taking advantage. The celebration was including the premiere of Harmony's new video too.

"All the sponsored posts are set to load at two p.m." Shell checked the clock. "So it should go live here in a second." She saw the clock turn to 1:55.

"Who all chose to sponsor?"

Hannah hadn't thought to ask those questions when the record company had come to her and told her they were allowing other artists to share her video release. She'd been so touched she hadn't even thought to ask numbers.

"Between country, pop, and some rock," she quickly checked her sheet, "we have a total of twenty."

"Which is fucking unheard of," Jared griped as he sat across from her at the table. "I wanna be you when I grow up, with all that friendly support."

She threw a piece of paper at him. "Shut up. I've been gone a long time. I'm surprised one person even wanted to do it, even though I should have a gimme with you guys."

Stacey, who'd come in with the family, sat down next to her. "I'm scheduling their social media now, because they can't seem to trust other people and Shell wanted nothing to do with it."

Hannah threw Shell a look. "I have enough on my plate with you."

"I can say wholeheartedly you're the first and only post today for Black Friday." Stacey gave her a grin.

Hannah felt the love in the room. Her parents and Garrett's parents were outside playing with EJ. Stacey and Brad had made the trip out. Chris hadn't been able to, but he'd sent her flowers earlier in the day telling her how sorry he was. He was still working on bettering himself with school, and she couldn't fault him for that.

Brad had a seat next to Stacey at the table and scooted closer to her. "I have to say, I'm pretty damn excited to see the video myself. I was always kind of into your music before you even became a part of the family. I'm a fan here." He slung his arm around Stacey's neck.

Glancing around the room, Hannah saw Garrett wasn't in the vicinity. He'd been shooting glares at the couple all afternoon. It'd been enough to send her into a fit of giggles earlier. Big brother was not excited at all that Brad and Stacey were still together, but he'd been told to leave them alone by everyone.

"Okay, okay." Shell beat the table with her fist. "I just got the message. It's loaded. Get everybody in here!"

Would it be okay if she crawled under the table? Maybe watched it on her own in the other room?

Hannah wondered as people started crowding into the dining room. This was one of the most embarrassing situations she'd ever been in, and she wasn't sure why. Maybe it was because the song hit so close to home, it was so personal, and even though they were public figures, she wasn't used to putting their love on display.

She knew the video was sexy; they'd made sure of that by having Garrett with her. You couldn't see his face, but his tattoos were there, exposed by the short-sleeve shirt he wore. It was a straight-up love song, but not one that was slow; it was upbeat, with a pop edge to it. She'd written the song not long after the two of them had gotten together—if she could remember correctly it wasn't long after their Vegas trip. Listening to the lyrics, she was taken back to those first few weeks and months where her thoughts had been consumed by him. She'd loved his green eyes, the sparks that flew when they were around each other, his dimples, and the reckless nature of their love. Everyone had told her she should run as fast as she could, but she'd known he'd pull her right back.

One night they'd stood in the rain kissing, and the song had written itself in less than ten minutes when she'd gotten back to her hotel room. She'd never let anyone hear it until Kurt had pulled the frayed paper out of the back of her binder, and feeling the emotions swell as she watched the video, she was glad he had.

As the video came to a close, the two of them in the middle of the pedestrian bridge in Nashville and water pouring down over top of them, their lips meeting in the sweetest kiss, she knew she'd made the best decision of her life.

"It turned out good, huh?" Garrett put his arm around her neck, pulling her to him.

She leaned her head back against his chest, letting him kiss her cheek. "Anything with us turns out good, but yeah, it did."

Over dinner, the group sat at the table discussing how much they loved the song, the video, and the fact Harmony Stewart was back. In the middle of the conversation, Shell's phone dinged, and she grabbed it, glancing at the message.

"Three hours in, Han, and you're at three million views. Pre-orders for the album have started at iTunes, and you're on three different charts there. The all-genre, the country, and the pop. It's happening!"

Hannah took a drink of her wine. It was definitely happening, and the train would keep going until it came to a natural stop.

Chapter Eighteen

"Jared and I drove by last night. People were already lined up," Shell commented as she and Hannah made their way through downtown traffic onto Lower Broad.

"Last night?" Hannah questioned, a touch of amazement and awe in her voice. "So some of them have essentially been lined up for twenty-four hours?

Shell gave her friend an excited look. "Yeah, they're excited, Han."

"Oh God." Hannah could feel the nerves start to bubble in her stomach, but there was also a huge amount of excitement. "I can't believe how fast this shaped up." She grabbed her phone out of her purse, took a selfie, and posted it to her Instagram.

Ready for my show at the world famous @Tootsies! Hope to see as many as we can pack in there! #nervous #readytobeback #thankyouforwaiting #myhothusbandwillbethere #reapersgirl

She was still a little amazed things were happening so

quickly. Three days ago the record company had approached her with the idea for a free show. She'd been quick to agree because she'd seen the good things free shows had done for Black Friday. Within a day they'd secured the venue, and then they'd leaked it to radio stations. Hannah had posted a teaser on Instagram, and news of her comeback had started to spread. Now fans had been lined up for over twenty-four hours.

"Things happen fast. You know that as well as I do, but it seems like it's warp speed this time, right?" Shell jockeyed for a spot behind the venue. There were only a few parking spots left, and they were reserved for Hannah and her family members.

"You can say that again." She breathed deeply as she sat in the passenger seat. At home she'd gotten ready because she'd been too afraid to do so at the venue. All she had to do was change her clothes closer to stage time. "I'm really excited though. They let me pick my set list, so I'm doing all kinds of songs I haven't done in years. All my favorites from every album."

Shell grabbed her bag out of the back. "It's going to be weird hearing you sing songs that were written back when you were eighteen, and I haven't heard you sing in so long."

"Are you kidding? At rehearsal yesterday, I had to pull the lyrics up on my phone for a few," Hannah laughed. "I have to be honest with you. This feels good, but I'm scared too. I've been gone a long time. A lot of those insecurities are creeping up."

"You're gonna fill this place and tear the roof off of

it. Next week your album drops, and then off you go."

Back when she'd told Garrett she'd wanted to go into the studio, she hadn't thought it would be this easy. Not that it'd totally been easy, but it'd been easier than she imagined. With the help of Garrett, friends, and family they'd made it through this process almost unscathed as a family. The rest should be easy, she told herself. But she wasn't so sure.

"You're sure you don't mind keeping him tonight?" Garrett asked his mother- and father-in-law as he packed up EJ's bag. They would all be riding to the show and supporting Hannah together, but afterwards they planned on going out and being adults for the first time in a long time.

"We don't mind, and you know he loves sleeping over at the house." Robert grabbed his grandson up, holding him while Garrett finished doing stuff around the house and giving Havock some extra food.

"Can you make sure I put his ear pieces in there?" Garrett grabbed his wallet and car keys. "Hannah will kill me if he can't watch the show because I didn't bring ear protection."

"Got 'em." His mother-in-law held them so he could see.

"Alright, then we're good to go. You ready to go see Mama?" He grabbed EJ up in his arms, and they all made their way out of the house. They were trying to figure out seating arrangements in cars when his parents and the rest of the band showed up.

Garrett loved how excited everyone was; he'd even put on a Harmony Stewart shirt like he'd worn back in the day, but this one was a little bigger than before. If he was going to wear it all night, he needed to make sure it wouldn't cut off his circulation. EJ wore one too, and all his bandmates out in California had taken a picture wearing one, showing their support earlier in the day. When they'd posted it to their Instagram account, he'd almost cried from laughing. It was one thing for him to show his support wearing a ridiculous shirt, but for them to do it—well, it said a lot about his friends. This show was important to her, and with it being on Lower Broad in downtown, where all the industry people were and the most die-hard of her fans, he wanted to show his support. He hoped she got a little laugh out of it too.

"We need to get going," he tried to rally everyone up. If he didn't they'd still be there well after Hannah went on, trying to figure out who was riding where.

"I'll make this easy." Jared raised a hand. "My wife drove his wife, so we need to ride together. We'll get the kid, and the rest of you can follow in two vehicles. We can get everybody back home, but we need to make sure the grandparents can take EJ home. Done?" He clapped his hands. "Done. Let's go!"

As the three guys got into Garrett's Range Rover, he looked over at his friend. "Thank you for taking control of that mess out there. Han would be so fucking heartbroken if we were late, and I could see it happening."

"Not a problem. Sometimes it helps not to be related to anyone."

Garrett had to agree with that one hundred percent. "Alright, everybody smile." Jared leaned in, and Garrett made sure to get EJ in the back in his car seat as he took the selfie. He'd seen earlier where Hannah had taken one, and he wanted to do the same for her.

On our way to see Reaper's Girl @harmonystewart perform tonight. If you're in Nashvegas and you're able to come to the show, be sure and do it. She practiced yesterday and I have to say, it was magic seeing my wife on stage again. #luckyman #groupie #marriedandhappy

"Your hashtags are killing me." Jared laughed as he glanced at the app on his phone.

"Ha! The married and happy is a stab at a website that posted this God-awful picture of me. I'm pretty sure it was after we did Crossfit, and they talked about how unhappy I looked. Well yeah, duh. I'd just puked my guts out, and they were saying there was trouble in paradise."

"I don't see how you two put up with that shit all the time." Jared shook his head. "It pisses me off for you."

"We hardly ever pay attention to it," Garrett admitted. "But that one in particular irritated me because could they not tell I'd just left my guts in the toilet? I mean really?"

"At least those of us around you know you're genuinely happy."

Garrett smiled widely, looking back at his son. "I am.

Way happier than I ever thought I could be, way happier than I deserve to be. But it's work. What a lot of people don't see are the sacrifices and decisions we make. Only you see a part of it too."

"It's why I always come to you for marital advice."

"I hardly ever know if I'm truly doing anything right, but when Hannah grins at me and tells me she loves me, I know I've done good things in another life or something."

They were both quiet as they approached Lower Broad, both trying to see what the line looked like and caught up in their own thoughts. "Holy fuck," Garrett breathed.

EJ in the back answered with his own *fuck*. Jared laughed, his own mouth hanging wide open as they saw the line of people waiting to get in to see Harmony Stewart.

"They do know they're only letting five hundred in, right?" Jared took a picture, sending it to Shell and Hannah.

"Maybe they're hoping they'll let a few more slip by. Shit, they even have the road blocked off." Garrett kept going through though, stopping when he got to a policeman. The cop walked up, recognizing him immediately.

"Hi, Reaper, if you turn left at the light and go through the back alley, they have parking for you and three other vehicles. Are the three behind you with you?"

"Yes, sir, they are. Thank you for making this such an easy process."

"No problem." The cop grinned. "My wife is in line to see Harmony tonight."

"Which one is she?" Garrett asked as he scanned the line.

The young cop turned around, doing his own scan until he found who he was looking for. "The cute redhead with the ripped jeans and Harmony shirt on."

Garrett spotted her quickly because there weren't many redheads in the line. He would make sure she got in and had a good time. "We'll take care of her tonight then. Thanks for your service." Garrett reached out and shook the man's hand before he made his way into the designated parking area.

"Shit's about to get crazy," Jared reminded him as they sat in the SUV, waiting for everyone to arrive.

"And need I remind you, crazy is what we thrive on. I don't know about you, but I'm excited."

Truer words had never been spoken. He was ready to watch his queen take her place in the spotlight again. Nothing would make him happier, and nothing made him more scared at the same time.

Chapter Nineteen

"Garrett posted on Instagram. They're on their way."

Hannah wasn't sure for whom she said the words – herself or everyone else. She needed to see her husband and friends, needed to see EJ. It wasn't like he would understand what in the world was going on, but she wanted him to be a part of it. It made her proud to know he'd be able to see her life—even if he wouldn't remember.

Garrett grounded her like no one else, and she wanted to see him, feel his warmth, and smell the cologne he knew she liked him to wear. She had never wanted to do this journey on her own and it meant the world to her he was going to be here and bring everyone with him.

"They just pulled in," Shell told her as she stuck her head in the door opening.

She closed her eyes and thought about how she felt at this moment. In this moment, she felt as special as she ever had. If she listened hard enough, she could hear them start to let in the fans, and she could almost sense their excitement. She'd changed a little while ago, and she wore her leather leggings, high-heeled boots, and the Reaper's Girl shirt Garrett had given her so long ago. Her hair was curled into corkscrews and her makeup was dark.

"I feel like we're having a déjà vu moment." Garrett came through the door holding EJ, taking in her look.

"Kinda does, doesn't it?" She laughed as she saw the shirt he wore. "Almost like we're having more than one. I can't believe you're wearing that shirt again."

"We have a history together." Garrett motioned for her to turn around before handing their son off to his mother-in-law.

"We do." She let him look his fill before she reached up and put her arms around his neck. "Who would have thought that when we first met? Who in the arena the night I went on stage with you could have predicted we'd be here now?"

That was easy—no one. They'd amazed people when they'd gotten together, and most everyone had assumed they get sick of each other quickly. They'd broken all the rules and were thriving together with their little family.

Grasping her around the waist, he pulled her into him, his gaze locking with hers. Garret stared at her for so long, she wondered if something was wrong. "What?"

"God, I did." He breathed the words out. "I didn't know exactly how much I would love you, but I knew we'd be together."

"I didn't know how much I would love you either, but standing here right now, I know exactly how much I love you." Her voice was soft because of the emotion she was feeling. Everything she'd worked for in the past few years was coming to fruition. Letting go of her career and having the family she'd always wanted was bringing her to the most beautiful place she'd ever been.

"I love you a fucking hell of a lot." He grinned.

"I love you just as much," she answered back.

Garrett let his thumb caress her cheek. "Still can't make you say it, huh?"

"No." She shook her head, smiling up at him.

He leaned in, his words a whisper. "But I can sometimes."

Her body warmed because she knew exactly the situations to which he was alluding. It took a lot for her to forget her morals and her upbringing. So far Reaper had been the one to do it. Part of her couldn't wait for him to make a comeback, the other part questioned whether she could handle it or not.

"Only you." She stood on her tiptoes, kissing him softly on the mouth.

Their lips mingled for longer than was proper, but by now their friends and family were used to their public displays.

She disentangled herself from him, trying to spot Shell. When she did, she waited until her friend saw her before she asked, "Are they letting the fans in yet?"

"They'll start in five minutes. Security is tight, so we may have to push the start of the show back about ten minutes."

That was fine with her. It would give her more time

to prepare, more time to be with her family and figure out what in the world she wanted to say to people she hadn't performed in front of in almost two years. EJ broke away from his grandma making a beeline to her. As she saw his little feet running towards her, she knew the decisions she'd made had all been good. Now she hoped this one was just as good.

"Are you ready?" she asked EJ, holding him on her hip.

He wasn't old enough to remember Black Friday's last concerts, and in the grand scheme of things, he wouldn't remember this one either. But it was important to her for him to be there, that he be a part of what was going on with them. When she'd started the journey, she'd worried constantly he would feel as if he was taking a backseat. It was obvious he hadn't; Garrett had done a terrific job in her place, but it still gave her pause.

EJ clapped his hands. "Ready!"

"They're starting to let people in," Shell informed the crowd hanging around.

In minutes they could hear the people who had gathered for the concert. They were loud as they waited. It sounded like someone had a speaker and they were playing Harmony Stewart songs while everyone waited.

"This is surreal." Hannah had to choke back emotion. When she'd said goodbye at her last concert, she'd meant it. She hadn't been sure she'd be back. At that point in time, she'd been so convinced all she'd ever want to do was be with Garrett, and that concert had truly been her stepping away point.

Now they'd grown up as a couple, their family had grown, and they'd watched some of their friends tour with children and make their situations work. Then her dreams had changed, they'd evolved into whatever this was. It all scared her, but she knew she had to try. It wouldn't happen just because she wanted it to.

"They're waiting on you," Shell told her thirty minutes later as they got the all-clear they'd let in the amount of people they were allowed to by the fire marshal.

"Are we ready?" she asked her band. The rehearsals they'd had were good, but she knew they would all be rusty until they got out there and fed off the crowd.

With everyone behind her, she went to the side of the stage and waited as she was introduced.

The roar of the crowd was enough to knock her down as she walked to center stage, her legs shaking, her knees knocking. Hannah had never been so nervous in her life, but it was at that moment Harmony showed up, and her hand didn't even shake as she brought the mic to her mouth.

"Hey, y'all!"

The crowd on the floor waved at her, catcalled, and welcomed her back with such enthusiasm she wanted to cry. Letting them get it all out for a few minutes, she put her mic down to her side and absorbed everything, taking it all in. "I've been gone for a little while, but I appreciate you coming here tonight to let me shake the dust off a little. If you'll notice, there's some cameras around. It's bein' filmed to be on TV in a few weeks, so let's all hope the band and I can get through this without screwing up too badly."

They laughed at her willingness to poke a little fun at herself.

"Tonight I'm gonna play you all my favorite songs from every album, including the new one, and if we're all good, maybe I can get my husband to come out and sing with me. He's wearing the most amazing shirt ever." She pointed to him. "It's got my face on it." She laughed.

Garrett stepped out from the wings, waving to the crowd and taking a bow. Loud applause went up as they saw his shirt. It was obvious the crowd loved her as much as he did.

"So without making you all wait any longer, how about we get into the first song."

Those words were met with loud applause, screams, and the stomping of boots on the hard floor. They were ready, she was ready, and with everyone behind her there would be no stopping her. It had taken everything leading up to this moment to remind her of who she was and what she stood for to every person out on the floor tonight.

Opening her mouth, she hit the first note, and she knew without a doubt Harmony Stewart was back.

Chapter Twenty

"Y'all are so loud I'm not sure you can even hear me." Harmony laughed as she took a break in between songs. Reaching into the people pressed up against the barrier, she shook as many hands as she could before going back towards the band.

It was hot on the small stage, and she fanned her face as she walked around, waiting on Jared to bring the stools out. As she waited, she glanced around the room, amazed once again that the place was filled front to back. There wasn't a spot in the room to even stand, much less get comfortable. Nobody was complaining though; everyone seemed to be having a wonderful time. It was as if leaving for a while had made her in higher demand. That'd never been her intention, but it was an interesting side effect of taking time off.

"Is it okay if I slow it down for sec?" she asked, smiling when the crowd gave a huge chant of affirmation that they were in fact okay with it. She kept speaking. "Y'all know my husband and I did a song a few years ago. I only sing it in concert if he's with me and vice versa. Luckily he's here tonight." She motioned for him, Jared, and Shell to make their way onto the stage.

The crowd exploded again as they saw Reaper walk from the wings, wearing his Harmony shirt. He flashed them a smile before he strode over to his wife, giving her a kiss on the cheek. As always, her heart skipped a beat. He was so hot when he was on stage. He didn't even have to sing; it was the way he moved like he owned it. No matter the crowd, he always had them in the palm of his hand and they would bend to his will. She loved singing with him.

"Thanks for having me out." He took her hand in his, leading her over to where Jared had put the stools.

"Thank you, Jared." She grinned over at him.

The crowd roared their approval because they knew about the cute little backstory of Jared always providing her a place to sit. "Like I keep telling you. I've been getting him laid since 1999," he replied.

She laughed, shaking her head. Couldn't take either of them anywhere, but she was so happy to be back onstage with her family, it didn't matter they were crass.

"Okay, we're gonna need some help with this one," she encouraged the crowd to sing along.

And sing along they did, almost drowning the group of them out as they harmonized on the chorus. Garrett reached down, kissing her as they finished singing. Squaring her shoulders, she turned around to face the room again. They only had a couple more songs, but everyone in the place tonight had learned something— something that would be spoken often when people asked about this show and how it went.

Harmony Stewart was back, and it was like she'd never left.

Chapter Twenty-One

"You're sure it's okay to leave him with you tonight?"

Hannah bit her thumb as she questioned her parents one last time. She helped her mom strap EJ into his car seat, handing him his favorite toy. A part of her wanted to go out and have a great time with her husband and friends, but there was another part of her that felt as if she were shirking her responsibility. It tore at her, sending her son with them while she and Garrett planned to have an adult night out. The logical part of her brain knew she had to take the time when she could. With the upcoming tour, date nights would be few and far between. It wasn't exactly easy to schedule babysitters on the road. Everybody had a job to do, and she hated to ask anyone to take time away from their own responsibilities in order to take care of something that was hers.

"He'll be fine," her mom assured her. "You can come get him whenever you want to tomorrow. We'll be up early, I'm sure."

Garrett leaned in, kissing his son's forehead, and

reached around Hannah's waist to grab her. His fingers were strong against the muscles of her abdomen. Taking the opportunity, she entwined them together, holding tightly. "C'mon, babe, he'll be fine. He's almost out already. He won't even know we're gone."

It was true, his head lay sideways against the back of his car seat, and his eyelids were fluttering as he listened to the commotion going on around him. Even the pacifier he loved to keep in his mouth was hanging haphazardly; he was close to the deep sleep that seemed to claim all children.

"Okay." She breathed deeply, knowing she and her overprotective nature were becoming too overbearing. If she held him too close, he'd never be able to experience all the things other kids did. She refused to let him live in a bubble just because of who his parents were. "I'll see you tomorrow."

They quickly said their goodbyes, leaving Garrett and Hannah alone with one another. Hannah watched the brake lights of her parents' car until she could no longer see them anymore.

"You ready to go have a good time?" he asked, brushing his nose against her neck, letting his lips slide down the smooth column of her throat.

She'd taken a quick shower and changed after the concert. Instead of feeling weary after giving her all for the past two hours, she felt refreshed and more full of life than she had in a very long time. "I'm ready." She smiled back at him. Maybe she did need a little grown-up time more than she cared to admit.

"Then let's get this show on the road."

Clasping hands, they walked to their SUV. It felt good to have her hand in his big one again. If there was one thing she missed when they weren't together, it was the small touches. The small touches did her in and made her fall in love with him all over again.

Garrett kept his arm around Hannah's waist as they made their way into the Nashville club. Shell and Jared had gotten there an hour before, grabbing them some seats in the VIP area. People stopped them every few feet, praising Hannah for the show she'd put on, letting her know how excited they were she was back, and all the good things they'd heard about the album.

"There they are," she shouted over the pulsing beat of the song playing over the sound system.

He helped her make her way through the packed house. Even the VIP area held an over-abundance of people. Many had heard this was where she would be going after her concert, and obviously they'd wanted the chance to see her. As they approached their friends, she had a seat next to Shell while he shook hands with Jared.

"You good?" he asked his friend, who sat with his arm around his wife's waist. A couple years ago, they would all be worried about him being in the presence of alcohol and whatever else the dark corners of this club held. Nobody had been able to trust him, and with good reason.

Jared tipped his head up to Garrett, nodding. "You

know I'm good. As long as you all are here this scene doesn't bother me."

It was a relief to hear after all the issues Jared had gone through the past few years. Plus, tonight, Garrett didn't want to be on alert for his friend, he wanted to enjoy the night, possibly one of the last nights they'd have alone in months.

"You want a drink?" he asked Hannah.

Her eyes widened with relief at his question. "Please, it's been a stressful day."

He leaned down, giving her a quick kiss as he made his way to the bar. Random people high-fived him as they first noticed his shirt and then recognized who he was. It didn't bother him here, not like it did in California, not like it did in other random parts of the country—he truly felt at home here.

Finally making his way to the bar, he ordered both him and Hannah a couple of drinks, and then took them back, again weaving his way through the maze of people. Hannah and Shell were laughing as he had a seat and handed her the glass of alcohol.

"I was so worried no one would show up, and then when I walked out onto the stage and I saw it was standing room only, I didn't know whether to laugh or cry." There were slight tears in her eyes now, and Garrett wondered if maybe she had cried, but hid it so no one could see. That was definitely the way of his wife, emotional sometimes to a fault, but honest about her reactions in most everything.

"Either way," Garrett took a drink, relishing the feel

of the warm alcohol making its way down his throat, "you killed it. From our perspective it looked like everybody was having an amazing time. Hell, I had an amazing time."

"I did too. I was worried I'd feel weird since it'd been so long, but it was like riding a bike. I loved being on that stage, and I realized how much I'd missed it."

Everyone who sat with her knew what a huge admission those words were. At one point, Hannah had hated the stage. It'd stifled her, and she'd wanted to get as far away from it as she could. To know she was coming around like this was a good thing.

Garrett glanced around at their friends and at the crowd. The one thing he wanted most in the world was to get his wife alone, but he didn't want to have to take her back to their house to do it. He loved showing her off, loved having her on his arm; the more public the setting, sometimes the more he liked it. There had been many people who said they'd never make it, who said they were too different and their marriage would be over in months. He loved that he could flash them a middle finger and prove to them he and Hannah still had it together. They would have it together for years to come because he knew he couldn't live without her.

And right now he wanted to show her off, wanted others to kind of see what he had but not be privy to it. A thought sprang to his mind. It wasn't often he asked her, and it sure as hell wasn't something he did on a regular basis. Knowing sometimes you did things for your spouses you wouldn't normally do, he leaned over and couldn't believe the words that came out of his mouth.

"I'd like to put my arms around you and hold you close. Do you wanna dance?" Garrett asked, grabbing her hand. He pulled his bottom lip between his teeth waiting for her answer.

Her eyes showed her surprise at his question, and the smile she gave him made his heart stop. "Yes, I'd love to!"

Chapter Twenty-Two

Hannah held tightly onto Garrett's hand as he directed them to a dark corner of the club. Here, they could hide their faces and bodies and hope no one would recognize a couple enjoying each other's company.

"Did you really have fun tonight?" he asked, his voice deep and loud in her ear as he leaned against the wall for stability.

They swayed to the beat; she let him hold her up. "I did." She leaned in close so he could hear her. "I forgot how much I missed it, how much it makes me get that adrenaline rush."

She felt his hands slip up her thighs, up under her skirt, pulling her closer to his body. They were in the dark, so she allowed it, separating her thighs so she could straddle one of his. "I understand." He kissed along the pulse point of her neck. "I only get that same adrenaline rush from you. You and the stage make me hard."

The drink she'd had earlier loosened her lips. "You and the stage make me wet," she admitted.

He wove a spell around her body, making her want nothing more than to be alone with him. Yet here they were, out here in the open, about to behave like teenagers. She gripped his shirt in her fingers, pulling him into her.

His mouth found the skin of her neck, nipping and soothing as one hand tangled under the nape of her neck, his fingers threading through her hair, the other moving further up the back of her thighs until they encountered the lace of her panties.

She wondered if he dare do it here, if she wanted him to. It struck her as odd, how much she'd changed from the girl she'd been when they first got together. That girl lurked under the surface sometimes, but for the most part Hannah Thompson was now a woman who knew what she wanted. "Do it," she encouraged him when she felt the tips of his fingers slip beneath the fabric covering the lower portion of her body.

He groaned deeply in her ear, the sound causing goosebumps to pop all over her body. "You sure?"

She nodded, nosing her way to his neck, kissing him hungrily, grabbing at the flesh there. "Do it before I change my mind."

Garrett had never disappointed her and he didn't now as he thrust two fingers deeply inside her body. Thank God he was leaning against a sturdy structure because her knees gave out and she sagged against him.

"Just let go." He breathed against her ear, capturing her earlobe in his mouth, using his teeth to tug on the sensitive skin.

His fingers in her hair tugged her to his liking and left her exposed so he could do whatever he wanted to her. Hannah gave herself over to him, letting him play her like he sang a song. It was intense, beautiful, and passionate all at the same time. There was no other man she'd ever give herself over to like this, and she knew that more now than she'd ever had.

She ground her hips against him, trying to get closer, one hand caught behind his neck, the other caught his hip, and she almost took her feet off the floor, leaving herself impaled on his fingers. He flicked against her, rubbing his palm against her sensitive clit. If it hadn't been with him, she would be embarrassed at how fast she exploded against him.

"Oh yeah, baby," he encouraged, feeling the rush of moisture against his hand, feeling the tightening of her body and then the relaxation of the aftermath.

He gripped her thigh with the hand that had just been shoved between her thighs, and shoved his cock up in between those same thighs. She hadn't even realized he'd unzipped, but as they ground against each other, she was thankful they were in a corner that was pitch black.

Hannah felt his sharp teeth against her shoulder as she felt him spill into her body.

"I'd be embarrassed if you hadn't come as quickly as I did," he spoke into her ear, his breathing choppy and uneven.

Hannah pulled back from him, not sure what had gotten into the two of them. Situating her skirt back around her thighs, she did her best to stand on her own two feet.

"What the fuck did we just do?" he asked, not believing it himself.

She giggled then, unexpectedly. "I can't believe it." She pushed her hand over her mouth. "You're a bad influence."

"Me?" he questioned as he zipped back up and adjusted. "You're the one who told me to do it." He pulled her close. "That's the hottest thing we've ever done, but let's not make public sex a habit, okay?"

She agreed one hundred percent, but with Garrett, hardly anything was out of the question.

"Your phone is blowing up," Garrett yelled at Hannah the next morning.

They'd gotten themselves up and dressed ready to hit a local pumpkin patch after they picked up EJ. He patted his thigh, calling for Havock. "You wanna go with us, boy?"

The dog loved to do anything with the family. It was as if he truly was a part of the family and understood everything going on. Garrett grabbed a bag that had the things they'd need for both Havock and EJ before he grabbed Havock's leash.

Hannah ran into the kitchen, putting her hair up in a ponytail. She looked like a teenager today. Her face was makeup free, hair up, wearing a pair of torn jeans and a long-sleeved shirt that read "the struggle is real".

"They started ticket sales today," she explained as

she sat down to put on a pair of shoes. "They're selling them all today. I think sales are gonna suck with them doing that, but the record company said it would be a good idea. I mean what if I sell nothing." She shrugged. "Okay, I take that back. I know I'll sell here, but the other stuff, I'm scared they're gonna cancel the tour." She laughed.

She never got the grasp of how big she was, and Garrett was kind of happy for that, because it meant she was always thankful for everything she had. He knew without a doubt the tour would sell out; the song was already a number one on the country chart and in the top ten on the pop charts. Something told him this would be the one show nobody wanted to miss.

"Well, why don't you grab your phone and see what the hell's going on. While you were getting ready it almost fell off the counter."

She rolled her eyes, giving him a face as she grabbed her phone. Putting in her passcode, he watched as her eyes read over whatever it was that had been sent to her. Her face changed and he got scared as he watched her eyes widen and a hand fly to her chest.

"Hannah?" he questioned, immediately worried.

"No, I'm okay," her voice was breathless as she spoke. "I just can't believe it."

"Believe what? You're starting to scare me."

She turned the phone so he could see what she was talking about. "The tour, in the first hour, has sold out over seventy-five percent of the dates." She stopped for a moment. "This is unheard of in country, Garrett, not unless you're a huge name."

"You are a huge name, babe. Maybe you'll realize that now." He scooped her up in his arms, twirling her around the room.

"They're asking if they can add some more dates in the bigger markets. Two days have sold out in some of them."

"Babe, go for it." He kissed her deeply. "I'm so fucking proud of you."

She was proud of herself too, but there was a part of her already feeling anxiety creeping in. "I'm nervous."

"You'll be fine, Hannah. We'll all be there with you, and we'll live this with you. You won't be by yourself, I promise."

She knew he spoke the truth, knew she didn't have to worry about the situations and scenarios she'd worried about before. Now however, it felt as if she had a whole new set of anxieties to worry over. She tried hard to push them down and be excited about what was going on in her life.

"Let's go get our son. I think Havock's ready." She pointed to the door where their dog stood holding his leash in his mouth.

Garrett threw his head back laughing. "Obviously he's sick of our shit."

"Obviously," she agreed dryly.

"Is that the one you want?" Hannah asked EJ as they walked through the pumpkin patch.

He'd loved everything they'd done. They'd played on the playground, gone to a petting zoo, and he'd tried his first cider slush. Havock ran ahead of them with Garrett, enjoying being out in the open. Overall, they were having an amazing family day.

"Yeah," EJ answered, shaking his head. "Dis one." He patted the pumpkin that was bigger than him.

"We gotta get daddy to come get it," she told him, scared she wouldn't be able to hold it and their son both. "Garrett!" she yelled. She didn't want to leave the pumpkin unattended in case someone else decided it would fit their family as well. It made her nervous to yell his name out like that in this hugely populated place. Because of the day, he wore his sunglasses and he'd pushed his long-sleeved shirt up above his elbows. He looked exactly how he did on stage, except he held a dog on a leash. He heard her the second time she yelled, and she was relieved as she motioned for him to come back to where they stood.

"This is the one he wants." She pointed to the large pumpkin.

"Holy crap." Garrett caught himself before he said the other word. "Let me go get a wagon. I have no doubt I can carry it, but it'll be awkward."

He leaned down, holding his hand out for his son. "Give me a high-five. You picked out a good one, EJ. It'll look good on the tour bus. We needed a big one for that."

As Garrett left with Havock to get a wagon, it struck her with clarity he was right. They would have this pumpkin on a tour bus, and whether she was ready for it or not, their life was about to get a lot crazier.

She picked EJ up, kissing him on the cheek. "Oh, I hope you're a good tour baby." She whispered a quick prayer up to the Lord above and plastered on a bright smile as Garrett and Havock appeared with a wagon to transport the pumpkin.

Looking back, this would be the last normal day they had as a family for a while.

Chapter Twenty-Three

Hannah did her best to breathe through the anxiety she was feeling. It was always worse at the beginning of a tour, and this was no different. A few hundred tiny little things had gone wrong—from them getting the wrong color of confetti delivered, to the wrong flowers to give out to meet-and-greet winners. It wasn't like she was picky, but there were some things they'd planned, and she wanted those things to all go smoothly. Things had to be color coordinated, and there were fans coming that were allergic to the flowers that had been delivered. She wondered if she'd made someone very angry in a past life, because today was not the day she needed all these things to happen. One or two at a time would have been fine. All in one day? She needed a drink.

She'd been summoned to wardrobe only to find out her opening outfit wasn't finished, and they'd had to measure her one last time.

The day had turned into a major cluster, and if she was given to saying curse words, the ones she wanted to spew forth would make Reaper proud. As it was, she was saying them in her mind, and more than once, one had almost slipped out. She knew people made fun of her for not cursing, but it'd always seemed such a crass thing to do, and she'd been taught to be a lady. In her limited experience, most people could be dressed down just as easily without the use of four-letter words. Today though, she was *this close* to letting someone hear one of those famous words slip between her lips.

"Hannah, they need you in hair and makeup." Shell came to the backstage area, a notebook and a pen in her hand. She looked worse for wear too. She'd had to get loud with a beverage vendor and the ladies in wardrobe over the outfit. They both looked to be almost at the end of their ropes, and this was only night one.

Hannah breathed deeply. Wardrobe had needed her five minutes ago, and she had yet to eat lunch. "I'll be there in a sec," she yelled over her shoulder. What she really wanted was a few minutes of peace and quiet, and if she was a smoker, she'd love a cigarette. Alas, she wasn't a smoker.

As she was walking down the hallway, she heard *"Mommy"* and then the pitter patter of little steps running towards her. If anything could brighten her day, it would be this little guy and maybe a hug from his dad. She stopped, a smile spreading across her face.

"Be careful, EJ!" She heard Garrett warn him right as she turned around.

When she did, she saw something that made her heart stop and bile rise up in her chest. EJ's feet got tangled up, not used to running on a hard floor, and he tripped, smacking his body against the hard concrete with a sickening thud. It happened in almost slow motion. She stuck her hands out, wanting to catch him, but knew she was too far away. Right before her eyes, she saw it happen and couldn't do anything to prevent it. The sounds of the hallway went away, and all she could hear was the thud of his face hitting the floor.

"Oh my God, EJ!" she screamed as she sprinted towards him. He wasn't more than ten feet away, but as it registered with her son what he'd done, his heartbreaking wail echoed through the halls, reverberating with a loudness that radiated inside the walls of her chest.

She reached him first, even though she heard the loud footfalls of Garrett not far away, taking her knees so hard she heard them pop against the floor. It was a pain she never felt. She'd never run so fast in her life. "EJ." She breathed heavily, trying to hold her fear at bay. "Let me see," she cooed in as calm a voice as she could.

But he didn't want to let her see, he wanted to bury his head in her shoulder and cry out all his pain. Hannah fumbled around blindly, putting her hand up to his nose and pulling it away quickly, feeling nauseous when she saw the blood on her palm. "Garrett," she called to him, making his eyes meet hers as he looked around for someone to help them, her voice hoarse. Holding her hand up, she showed him the blood.

He reached them then, going down on his knee to kneel next to his wife and son. "C'mon, buddy, let me see." He was trying to coax his son to let go of his mom, but he grabbed harder around her neck and screamed in her neck.

"Is it his nose or his head or his lip?" he asked Hannah.

"I don't know." She rubbed her hand up and down EJ's back in the most soothing manner she could. "He won't let go of me, and I don't want to hurt him by making him let me see."

His wails were tearing at her heart. All she could hear was him screaming *Mommy* and then nonsensical mumblings. It scared her to death. She saw both Jared and Shell come running, their faces white as they took in the sight in front of them.

"What happened?" Jared asked, fear making his voice shake.

"He fell," Garrett explained, swallowing deeply against the knot in his throat. "Can one of you grab us a rag and the other go get medical for the venue?"

Hannah appreciated his calm voice of reason, because she felt like she was ready to melt down. How she was holding it together, she wasn't sure, but possibly this was what people meant when they said mother's intuition. Her hands shook as she stretched her legs out and sat against the wall, letting EJ lean against her. He was still screaming as she whispered soothing words in his ear. "C'mon, honey, let me see."

When he finally did, her heart started beating normally again as she saw he'd busted his nose and lip, but it looked like his teeth and head were fine.

"Garrett," she whispered, hoping not to scare their

son into burying his head in her neck again.

Blood poured from his lip, but that wasn't unusual. Garrett had a seat next to her. "Hey, little guy, let me see." He coaxed EJ to look over at him, lightly pushing EJ's lip up.

Shell arrived with a washcloth, letting Garrett take it from her. He started cleaning the blood from EJ's nose and lip, breathing a sigh of relief when he didn't think he saw anything broken. EJ was starting to calm down too; the tears were still streaming, but he wasn't sobbing and he could sniffle. That made Garrett feel better.

"What have we got here?"

The parents looked up as they saw a female EMT with a huge first aid kit hurrying towards him. Her eyes took in the scene quickly, and she had a seat with them.

"He was running towards me," Hannah explained. "His feet got tripped up, he hasn't been running that long, and he took a header into the floor."

The female EMT smiled at EJ, handing him a stuffed animal. "That's okay, we'll fix you up." She reached out, and EJ went willingly into her arms.

"Did he lose consciousness?" she asked the worried parents as she held the washcloth to his lip and using a penlight to look in his eyes.

"I don't think so," Hannah answered. "Almost as soon as he smacked the floor he started screaming bloody murder, and then he wouldn't let me see it, but I'm confident he didn't hit the top of his head, I think it was the middle portion."

"I think you're right," she agreed as she put the penlight down. "He's not exhibiting signs of a head injury." She felt along his hairline and his forehead. "And I don't feel any swelling."

"What about his teeth?" Garrett asked, asking the question she wondered about too.

"I think they're fine." She slipped her gloved finger up under his lip, feeling around. "I know it hurts," she soothed him as he pulled back. Lifting his lip up, she showed the two of them. "I think he cut his lip on his teeth, they aren't loose or anything." She tried to move them with her fingers. "I think he got really lucky."

Hannah sagged into Garrett, realizing their son had indeed gotten very lucky.

"He'll probably be bruised for a few days. I'd ice it to keep the swelling down. If you still have a teething ring, that would probably be perfect, and children's Tylenol for the pain."

"Thank you," Garrett told her. Picking EJ up, he breathed deeply into his son's head as EJ wrapped himself around his dad's body.

"No problem." She grinned. "That's what I'm here for." She paused. "Well, that and the concert."

Hannah grinned back at her. "I don't know how I'm going to get on that stage after I've been scared to death."

"You'll do fine and so will he. Kids are very resilient."

"Hannah, we really need you in hair and makeup."

It was on the tip of her tongue to tell them tough shit, she had a son who needed her, but she knew she had to work. "Will you be okay?" She pushed EJ's hair back from his forehead.

He shook his head, reaching out for her. Obviously when little boys got hurt, they just wanted their moms. She'd make this work because she knew she had to. They couldn't fail on the first night of the tour.

Shell appeared with a washcloth wrapped in ice. "Here ya go."

Hannah grabbed it, meeting Garrett's sympathetic eyes. This was what being a mother meant. "C'mon, EJ, wanna see what hair and makeup looks like?"

Later on, she shared a picture on her Instagram of her with her hair in rollers, her face halfway done, holding her sleeping son in her arms with an already bruising mouth and nose. She captioned it:

When your son scares you to death by falling on a concrete floor – opening night of the tour has to go on – as does being his mom. #momlife #tourlife #thankful #blessed

It wasn't a surprise to anyone that even though the day had started off with such a stressful situation, Harmony Stewart brought her A-game and delivered for a sold-out show of fans in Chicago.

Chapter Twenty-Four

"I'm not sure how we're going to keep up with all of these requests for your time we have. People want you on their magazines, they want sound bites, and they want interviews. It's fucking nuts." Shell ran her hand through her hair, blowing out a frustrated breath. "I feel like I need an assistant to be an assistant to you. This is a lot to keep up with, Han."

They'd always been honest with one another, even when it'd been hard to be, so Hannah knew Shell was telling her the truth.

"What's changed?" Hannah questioned, her face pensive as she and Shell went over her schedule. "Like, when did it get to be so much? I was never this in demand before; I kind of don't understand what caused it. I know I released a record, but I've done that before."

"Wanna know what I think?"

"You know I value your opinion probably more than anyone else's except for Garrett's, and sometimes yours is much more insightful than his is."

Shell paused for a moment, and Hannah knew she

was trying to form her words in a way not to cause more anxiety than Hannah already felt. "I think you taking your time off in order to have a family and then being so open—not only about the marriage, but the pregnancy too—has blown you into the stratosphere. Before people looked at you like you were this star who was so unattainable, and then you met a guy, fell in love, got married, and had a family. The two of you are living the American dream; it's what everyone wants, and you're doing it. I think it made so many people think you could be their best friend down the street, and now they all want a piece of you. You're doing so well right now because you're so well liked. This is organic, Han. Nobody's going to take it away from you."

That was the source of some of her anxiety, and both she and Shell knew it. She was worried it would all go away, including her husband and son, and she'd be left holding an empty life. The empty life she'd had before they came into it. It wasn't one she ever wanted to go back to. Looking at herself through the eyes she had now, she realized she hadn't even enjoyed it. It'd been about pleasing other people and not herself. It would be detrimental to her mental health to go back to that life now.

"I just keep telling myself this could all go away tomorrow, because that's what I've told myself the entire time I've been an artist, you know? You don't wanna get too comfortable where you are because one bad single, one bad shot, or one horrible article can ruin you forever. It's like I'm constantly waiting for the other shoe to drop, which I know is crazy, but the way this album has blown up, Shell. Can you blame me?"

Shell had to be just as honest. "No." She laughed. "In all the years we've been in this business together and seen overnight sensations happen, I've never seen this with anyone else. You're number one on three charts right now. The pop, country, and the adult contemporary. You've got all the basic bitches covered."

Hannah laughed so hard she almost cried. "I needed that. I start taking things too seriously, and then I get in trouble because I get too deeply inside my head. This is scary though, Shell, like when you're this big everybody wants to bring you down, and that worries me. I have a lot to lose: a family, a child, a career."

If people targeted her, it wouldn't be the first time, but she would not have EJ hurt because of how she chose to live her life. More than anything she worried people would make a spectacle of her son. He hadn't asked to be born into this lifestyle, and she constantly warred with herself. Did she allow the public to see him or not? In the end she decided to because this was her life, it's what she did, and no matter what, others would assume he would do it too.

"We're not gonna let that happen, Han. We'll accept the requests from the people we know and we'll tell the others to kiss our asses. We're only in week two of this tour, we can't burn out yet."

Hannah knew every word Shell said was right, but it didn't keep her from worrying.

"Are you sure you wanna come with me? It's just a radio interview," Hannah explained to Garrett.

EJ was with Jared for the afternoon, playing out some of his energy on a nearby playground, leaving Garrett alone for the time being. He hadn't been able to do any of the normal stuff with her because usually he watched their son. Today he wanted to be included. "Yeah, it'll be fun to see someone else get grilled."

She groaned because that was one of her least favorite parts of interviews. More often than not the radio DJ wanted to delve too deeply into her personal life. For a public figure, she thought she shared way more than necessary, hoping to make sure people didn't want to snoop. "Alright, we're leaving in a few minutes."

An hour later they were at SiriusXM Studios getting fit with mics and meeting the DJs who would be taking part in this town hall for the afternoon. Upon arrival, Hannah found out they were letting fans in to ask questions. As they were going over what was okay to ask and what was not okay, she felt Garrett stiffen next to her, and she heard a low curse.

"What?" she asked, trying to see what or who had caught his attention.

"Nothing," he shrugged it off, "just thought I saw someone I used to know."

She wanted to question him but couldn't as they had her have a seat and then welcomed the group of fans into the room. All through the Q & A session, she kept an eye on Garrett, noticing one of the female DJs not part of her session walking over to him. The DJ approached him and tried to hug him, but Garrett held her back, keeping his arms crossed over his chest as they faced off against each other.

Hannah tried to tell herself she wasn't jealous, she was just curious.

"The story of how you and your husband met, is it true? You met at an awards show?" one of the interviewers was asking.

Garrett's head snapped up and he met her gaze. She smiled at him. "It is. He told me to have a good show, and then I saw him again on the red carpet to the after party once it was done. We took a picture together, and I never realized how one picture could change your life. We've been together ever since."

"And you had a son almost two years ago?"

"Yeah." She grinned. "EJ is a handful, but he's enjoying the touring life right now. So far he's excited that he seems to get to go to every zoo and nearby playground all these different cities offer."

The crowd laughed, but she noticed Garrett didn't. His attention was still focused on the woman beside him. Jealousy was a foreign feeling for her. She'd never questioned Garrett's motives with other women— ever—but there was something about *this* woman she didn't like.

It was a struggle to get through the rest of the interview, and Hannah tried to act like she was paying attention, but all she wanted to do was rip the microphone off and ask Garrett who this woman was. She was still standing next to Garrett when Hannah concluded her commitments and made her way over to where they stood.

As soon as she was within arm's reach, he grabbed her in his arms, hugging her tightly to him, kissing her passionately. Hannah was as confused as she'd ever been. It wasn't like they hid their love or passion from people, but they normally weren't so completely open about it either.

"I was looking for you," she said as he pulled back. "But I saw you had a visitor."

Garrett looked like he didn't want to make the introduction, and in the end, he didn't. Hannah turned to the other woman, and when she did, the obviously not appreciative woman took her shot.

"Hi, Harmony. I'm a huge fan." She smiled brightly.

"Thanks," Hannah answered, not sure whether to believe her or not. "Nice to meet you…?" She purposely left off the name so she would have to be told.

"Vanessa, my name's Vanessa."

The Vanessa?

It took everything Hannah had to as polite to her as she could be. "Oh bless your heart, that's a beautiful name."

Garrett choked back a laugh and grabbed hold of Hannah. "We gotta go, babe. It's almost EJ's nap time, and you gotta get ready for the show."

As they left, Vanessa waved, telling Garrett how good it was to see him again.

Hannah didn't say anything, but when they got to the waiting SUV, Shell asked who they'd been talking to.

Without skipping a beat, Hannah glared at Garrett before speaking. "Vanessa of the Vanessa fame."

"Oh shit." Shell laughed. "You're in so much trouble, and you probably don't even know it."

"I didn't do anything," he argued.

"Do you have anything to reply to that, Han?" Shell asked, because she knew she did.

"I saw the way she was sidling up to you, trying to touch you, and trying to engage you in conversation. You're a married man for goodness sakes."

"Well, you did tell her to fuck off." Garrett laughed.

Shell whipped her head around, staring wide-eyed at her friend. "You did what?"

"I said *bless your heart* to her. I didn't come right out and say it. I wanted to though. She knew exactly who I was and still kept making googly eyes at *my* husband."

"Tell us how you really feel," Shell encouraged her.

"If she were a cookie she'd be a whoreo, and that's the last I'm saying on the matter unless she ever shows up again."

Garrett put his arm around her neck, pulling her deeply into his chest, laughing loudly. "You're cute when you're jealous."

Chapter Twenty-Five

Hannah was dragging after a training session with the personal trainer they employed on tour. Three weeks in and she could feel the effects, even though she was doing her best to stay on top of being healthy and well rested. Touring just wasn't a place conducive to those two conditions. Climbing onto the tour bus, gritting her teeth when she felt the pull in her glutes, she was met by EJ.

"Morning." She kissed his sleepy face, pushing his tousled hair back from his forehead. He still had a slight bruise on his nose, but for the most part, no one could tell he'd fallen so hard recently. He ate a banana, one of the only things he ate consistently, and held his hands up for her to lift him. His favorite thing to do after waking up was cuddle with her, and she had to admit it was her favorite too.

Picking him up, her thighs screaming, she made her way into the back of the bus, where Garrett was sitting on the couch, his cellphone at his ear. Havock was at his feet, glancing up at his owner.

"This wasn't what we planned."

Hannah felt bad for the person on the other end of the line. The tone with which he spoke to them was one hundred percent Reaper. She held EJ close to her, letting him munch on his banana as she listened to her husband. When she realized the call was getting serious, she grabbed the tablet they let EJ watch and turned on some cartoons for him so maybe he wouldn't pay attention to his dad.

"What am I supposed to do?" He huffed before he grit his teeth so hard that she heard his jaw pop. "You make the calls, right? It doesn't matter what I was promised or what I have going on in my life, does it?"

Her stomach pitched, and she suddenly got a very bad feeling about the conversation. Telling herself she wouldn't jump to conclusions, she curled up on the couch, holding EJ closer, kissing his forehead as he was content to hang out with her. Every once in a while her eyes would search out Garrett, and then she wished she hadn't. He looked angrier every time they made eye contract.

"I'm not sure I believe this fucking apology," he fired off the words into the mouthpiece of his phone. "You know the shit I have going on in my life right now, and the token *I'm sorry* I just got seems more like a great big *fuck you and your family*. But whatever." He ran his hand through his hair. "I'll make it work like I always do."

She watched as he swiped the screen, ending the call, and then promptly threw his phone across the room.

Thankfully, EJ was too engrossed in his show to worry about what was going on around him. It scared Havock though, who tucked tail and ran to the front of the bus.

"You okay?" Her voice was soft, like she was speaking to a wounded animal.

"I'm fucking pissed."

If she hadn't been able to tell by his actions or his tone, she could tell by the color of his face. It was blood red, and he held his bottom lip between his teeth, biting into it as he paced the room back and forth.

"Why don't you tell me what happened?" She shifted EJ off her, sitting him against the couch and covering him up with a blanket before standing and joining Garrett where he stood with his back to her.

Silently, she reached around his stomach, hugging him tightly before putting her cheek to his back. The anger and annoyance reverberated off him so hard she was afraid he'd shoot his blood pressure up. They weren't as young as they used to be anymore. "Calm down, Garrett. Whatever it is, we'll make it work," she soothed.

He was close to the opposite wall, and he leaned into it, propping his hand, letting his head fall on his shoulders before reaching down his stomach and grasping hers with his other. The tension was palpable within his body, and she wished there was something she could do about it. "Tell me," she encouraged him again. She couldn't make it better or make any plans if he wasn't going to be honest with whatever was going on.

"That was Rick. They want to move up our recording sessions. Before you came out on the tour, we busted ass to finish writing so I could concentrate on taking care of EJ while you worked. Since we finished, they want to expedite everything."

In the blink of an eye, Hannah came to the realization she'd always feared they'd come to. While having young children, there was going to be no way they'd be able to each have a career, and it would come down to who was willing to give theirs up, as far as touring and promotion went. "I don't know what to say," she admitted, kissing along the edges of his back.

"Oh I do." He formed a fist with his one hand and punched at the wall. "I'm so fucking pissed off." He shook his head. "We had this all planned out, had it all worked out—" He broke off, inhaling deeply. He finally turned around, his green eyes meeting her dark ones. "I'm so damn sorry."

"Garrett." She pushed her arms around his waist, holding on tightly. "This isn't your fault, not at all. Like you told him, we'll make it work." What she didn't add is they would never be in this situation again. After the tour, and save for the record that would finish out her contract with the record company, she wouldn't be putting them in this situation again. It was a no-brainer for her. Black Friday had a ton of people on their payroll. She had herself and Shell.

"I told you when you came to me and wanted to do this that I would support you and I would make it happen for you." He stopped again, not able to put what he was feeling into words.

"And you have." She reached up, mapping his face with her fingers.

He wore his glasses today, and he looked distinguished, but it also allowed her to see his eyes. They were tormented and unsure. She knew it killed him to disappoint her, and truth be told, it hurt for her too, but she also understood he had a contract to fulfill. The band had a contract to fulfill. No matter what, they were always at the mercy of the company holding that contract. *Until it was over.*

"When do you have to leave?"

The way his mouth twisted in a grimace, she knew she wasn't going to like the answer. "Rick's calling everyone else. They want us there in two days. We'll be recording in three."

Okay, that made her start to panic a little. How were they going to cram memories into two days? The rest of the tour was stacked and packed.

"Don't freak out on me," he begged her, holding onto her with his strong hands. "I know this isn't what either one of us had planned."

"Not in a million years," she admitted. "How are we going to make it without you?" She finally let her fear shine through. EJ loved his daddy, she loved her husband, and the fact of the matter was—they were strong as a family unit.

"You'll visit when you can, I'll visit when I can, and we'll make this work. Remember the early days when we were together?"

She did remember those early days. They were some

of her favorite memories, but at the same time, she'd hoped they'd never have to rely on FaceTime to see each other on a normal basis again. "We'll make it work," she decided, leaning in to give him a kiss.

"Please tell me we will," he whispered. "Please tell me you aren't mad at me."

"I'll never be mad at you for doing something you have to do, Garrett," she assured him. "Neither one of us can predict what the record companies are going to do until we've completely fulfilled our contracts with them, and looking back, we were naïve to think we could."

He crushed her to his chest, holding tightly as they were both quiet in their own thoughts. Hannah held on for dear life, more scared than she'd ever been. How in the world was she was going to make this work without him and with EJ? Obviously their son couldn't be around while they were recording an album. There was too much work to be done. He'd have to stay with her. Not to mention if she lost both of them? God, they might as well take a limb and her heart at the same time.

This tour had just gotten a lot more complicated, and it'd definitely made her vision much clearer about her future. For now she'd keep those decisions to herself and hope to God they could make it through the next six months.

Chapter Twenty-Six

"**P**romise me you'll be good for your mom," Garrett spoke quietly to EJ while Hannah did her best to hold back tears.

It wasn't like their almost-two-year-old understood what his dad was saying to him. He just knew his dad was being serious. She watched as EJ nodded solemnly, taking very much to heart what was being said to him.

The tears almost came gushing forth as Garrett hugged his son fiercely. He wasn't going to war, he wasn't leaving and never coming back, but knowing he wouldn't be there when she went to bed tonight was killing her. He let go of EJ, who ran over to be with Shell, and turned to face Hannah.

Seeing the despair on his face was all it took for her to sob. She hated this, hated the loneliness she already felt, the coldness his not being there would leave behind. Garrett held his arms out to her, folding her into his body, but that only made her cry harder.

"This is bad," she whispered as she twined her arms around his waist, burying her face in his neck. "I don't know what I'm going to do without you. I'm gonna call your mom and see if maybe she'd be willing to come out for a few dates, just so I don't leave EJ with Shell all the time." She was truly at a loss.

He hugged her so hard she worried he might crack her ribs, but at the same time she welcomed the show of emotion from him. Since they'd found out he would be leaving, he'd been stoic and unwilling to talk to her about it. They'd not argued, but they'd also not been their same fun-loving selves.

His voice was strained as he spoke. "You know I'm only a phone call, a FaceTime, a plane ride away. I fuckin' hate this." He threaded his fingers through her hair as he palmed the back of her skull.

"I do too." She grasped the back of his shirt in her hands as she hugged him tighter. Maybe if she held on, he wouldn't be able to go, she could force him to stay.

"Guys, it's time to go." Rick's voice was like a bomb in the quiet room. He'd come to make sure they were actually going to get on the plane.

Hannah pulled away, wiping at the tears on her face. "C-call me when you get there," she choked out.

Garrett rolled his eyes skyward, seeming to try and compose himself. "You know you're the first person I worry about."

She nodded, rising on her tiptoes to meet him as he dipped his head down. Their kiss was sweet, not holding the passion that usually gripped them as soon as their lips touched. This taste of each other held the tinge of sadness and the wish of not having to leave. She tasted salt and wondered if she were the only one crying or not.

Pulling back, she buried her head in his chest again. "You better go."

"I love you." He said the words fiercely, anger slightly on the edge, but she knew it wasn't directed at her, it was more at the situation.

"I love you too." She did, so much more than she ever thought she would. Watching him walk away would hurt more than she imagined. She knew without a doubt it would feel like a piece of her soul was missing until he came back. They weren't whole unless they were together.

Finally he released her and it caused her to stumble, but she caught herself against a chair sitting in the lounge.

"C'mere and give me a hug." He bent down to eye-level with EJ who, not knowing what was happening, ran to his dad full speed. "Remember what we talked about. We won't see each other for a while."

EJ babbled breaking Hannah's heart in the process because her son didn't understand, wouldn't understand until he wanted his daddy.

All too soon the guys were gone, leaving Shell, EJ, and Hannah standing alone. Shell reached over, grasping her friend by the shoulders as she sniffled herself. "This sucks." She blew out a long breath. "Just when I get really used to having him around."

"They up and have to leave again," Hannah finished for her.

"We're a pair—feeling sorry for ourselves like this."

Shell tried to laugh, but it came out as a sob.

"It's okay; we're allowed to be sad. They weren't supposed to be doing this for almost another year. Life isn't fair, and I understand that, but I want a normal life sometimes."

"You had it, remember? And then you decided you wanted to record again."

Hannah couldn't fault Shell for telling the truth, but now she wondered why she'd been so ready to get back on tour. Granted, she'd been bored, but being bored was way better than this gnawing emptiness she felt without Garrett.

"Tell Daddy good night." Hannah held EJ in her lap as the three of them FaceTimed together.

EJ babbled, not able to say those words yet. All he knew was he was excited to see his dad. Since they'd started the session, he kept reaching out, trying to touch him.

"Are you being good?" he asked EJ, who nodded. Even though he'd been in trouble twice that day.

"He's trying." Hannah kissed him on the cheek. "But right now I think he's tired. Shell's staying with us tonight, so I'm gonna go give him to her, and I'll be right back."

"Love you, EJ." Garrett waved sadly to his son.

"Love you!" EJ blew a kiss, and it tore Hannah's heart apart further.

When she came back, Garrett was waiting patiently.

"You look tired."

Hannah smiled. "I *am* tired. You know I don't sleep well without you, and EJ was okay the first two days, because I think he was assuming you'd be right back. It's a week now, Garrett, and I haven't slept good in almost five days."

He could feel the pressure tight in his shoulders and he hated it. He hated letting down his family. "Babe, I'm so damn sorry."

"It's not your fault," she cooed. "You have to do what you have to do, but I think it's time we have a talk about something."

Judging by the circles under her normally bright eyes, something more than EJ had been keeping her awake, and he wasn't exactly sure right now was the best time to be having any kind of conversation. Not when she was obviously fatigued and stressed. "Are you sure? I don't want you to say something you might regret later because you're tired."

"No I've thought about this—actually nothing *but* this for the past seven days, Garrett. First I need to tell you the record label asked me to extend the tour."

If it were possible for his stomach to evacuate his body through his feet, he was pretty sure it did just that. Her extending the tour would mean a myriad of complications for their lives, and for their son. "What did you say?" He was scared to death to hear the answer. A selfish part of him hoped she said no, the other part knew extending was a major accomplishment for her.

"I thought about it, along with everything I've been

thinking about since you left." She gave him a gentle smile. "As much as we wanted to convince ourselves we could do this—be in different genres and make a life as parents to a toddler work—I don't think we can."

"We can do anything we want," he argued.

"No you're right about that, we can, but at what cost? EJ not knowing one of us? Our marriage suffering?"

Frustrated, he set his phone down and took a deep breath. "Don't you think you're overreacting? It's been a week."

"A very long week," she whispered. "One I don't want to ever live again if we don't have to. The answer to our situation is simple."

He smirked. "Nothing with us is ever simple, babe."

She smiled at his affectionate tone. "This, in my mind, is very simple. You have a whole group of people to worry about. I have Shell and me. We've talked about it, the two of us, because this affects her as much as it affects me. We're pulling the plug after the final album is done. The record company agreed it could be a greatest hits, and after that I'm a stay-at-home mom and wife until EJ and any other children we have are of age."

He opened his mouth to cut her off, to ask questions.

"Wait, let me finish. That's not to say I won't record again, because I think I'll want to, but I'll record under my own label, and I won't tour. I may decide to do some festivals and private shows, but Garrett, we can't raise a family like this. Not with both of us on opposite sides of the country. You have to know I'm right."

He did know she was right, but it didn't mean he agreed with it. When she'd married him, he'd wanted her to have the same life she'd always had, he'd wanted her to have the world at her fingertips, and now he felt like he was holding her back. "I don't want you to wake up regretting it one day."

"Right now what I wake up regretting is that you aren't in bed next to me. EJ's looking for you every morning." She swallowed hard. "It's not like you're part of the military or you're away working because our family needs the money. If I can give up my career for a while to make things easier on our family it's a no-brainer, Garrett. I promise I know what I'm doing."

He hoped with everything he had she was right, because if the day ever came she resented him; he wasn't sure how he'd survive.

Chapter Twenty-Seven

Two weeks. Hannah checked off the dates on her calendar. It had been two full weeks since they'd seen the guys from Black Friday.

"Hey." Shell stuck her head into the room of the backstage area.

"Yeah?"

"I need to get out of here and get some sunshine and fresh air. If not, I'm gonna cry again. There's a park half a mile up the road. Do you care if I take EJ?"

This was another thing that bothered her immensely. Without Garrett around, she couldn't spend as much time with EJ as she wanted to, as much time as he needed. She'd tried telling herself she wasn't a failure, but she was beginning to feel like one.

"Yeah, make sure he wears his jacket though." They'd rolled into the northeast, and being October, it was starting to get colder. The last thing she needed was for EJ to get sick.

"Will do. We'll be back in about an hour and a half. Try and get some rest."

Hannah wished she could, but she hadn't rested well since Garrett had left. There was something uneasy tingling at the back of her mind. She wasn't sure what the feeling was, but she didn't like it at all. In the years since she'd been with Garrett, she'd started to be more confident in herself, so the doubts she was having right now were very foreign to her. Blowing out a breath, she picked up a piece of paper, wadded it up, and threw it. Frustration ate at her.

Grabbing her phone, she started to check her email when a headline caught her attention.

Black Friday at SiriusXM studios today. Are Reaper and Harmony Over?

Hannah sighed, fuming as she opened the page. Her hands were shaking as she saw the picture with the article. He stood with his arm around Vanessa, a smile on his face. The sinking feeling in her stomach made her angry. She'd never doubted him before. Not once. Not even when those pictures had come out of him and that girl when he'd gotten drunk with the band. *These* pictures, though, they stung a lot, and the words written in the article? They struck a nerve.

Has Reaper left his wife and son to rekindle and old flame while she's out on the road and he's left at home to play?

Before she could talk herself out of it, she screenshot the pictures and sent them over to him with a message. Her fingers flew furiously over the keyboard on her phone.

Thought you couldn't stand being around her. You seem pretty chummy right now.

Knowing the time difference where he was at, she didn't expect a quick answer, but as she sat her phone down, she had a message from Garrett.

Wtf? Are you kidding me right now? This is business.

She was feeling meaner than she had in a while; her exhaustion and frustration got the better of her when she fired off the next text.

The same way Bryson and I were business? I seem to remember you reacting badly to that whole situation.

A FaceTime request came in, and she ignored it. The rational part of her brain told her this was stupid. They hardly ever argued, and when they did, they didn't get nasty with one another. She had no idea what was happening right now. The only thing she knew for sure was she wanted him as angry as she was.

Really? You're gonna fucking play like that, Han? You won't answer my fucking FaceTime? What in the fucking hell is going on with you right now? We're married – she's a worker at a place where I was doing my job – I can't even fucking deal with you.

She took exception to the number of times he used the F-word in the text message. Tears pricked the edges of her eyes because she hated fighting with him, but she was angry and jealous, and she wanted to be the person he stood with his arm around. Her fingers shaking, she went about composing another message to him, throwing in her own F-word for the sake of argument.

Ya know what? I can't even fucking deal with you either and do you know what it makes me feel like to see a woman who's slept with you that close to you when I haven't seen you in weeks? You had a smile on your face, Garrett, and the last time you saw her, when I was with you I might add, you looked like you wanted to maim her. It doesn't feel good. Don't you think she knows what she gave up? Don't you think she realizes the kind of man you are now?

Minutes passed, and she'd almost given up on him texting her back.

Babe, don't you realize how much I love you?

The tears started, and they wouldn't stop. Who was she to be going off like this? What was this fit of jealousy? It wasn't like her. As she thought about what she wanted to say, another message came through.

You have nothing to be jealous of. I miss you as much as you miss me.

She sniffled, holding her breath before her shaking fingers began to compose another message.

This is so hard. I miss you, EJ misses you, Havock

misses you, and I don't understand why we keep doing this to ourselves.

She waited a long time for his next text, and she wondered if he had to get control of himself too. Setting the phone down beside her, she shoved her face in her hands and sobbed, loud, wracking sobs. The stress of everything was getting to her, and the one person she counted on to help her through it all wasn't there. Finally, her phone dinged a text from him.

You have three days off in a row after this concert. Come see me, even if it's only for a few hours.

Doing the math in her head, she realized it would only be for roughly a day in a half, but it would be worth it. She missed him, EJ missed him, and she felt like she couldn't breathe without him around.

Let me see what I can do. I love you

The words were the easiest she'd ever said. She *did* love him, no matter what, and that's what made every part of the situation they were in right now so difficult. What made her angrier than anything was knowing she could have prevented it – if she hadn't decided to give it a go and stretch her boundaries.

I love you too, babe. You know I'll do whatever it takes to make this work. I'm sorry seeing that picture of us together got you upset, it was never my intention. And hey, next time I FaceTime, pick it up. I miss your face.

The laugh that bubbled up for her throat was watery at best.

I miss your face too.

In the background, she could hear the sound of EJ's shoes stomping against the floor of the hallway, and she did her best to clean up the remnants of the tears. Putting on a happy face, she hoped neither he nor Shell could see she'd been upset.

"We're sufficiently worn out now," Shell heaved as she launched herself onto the couch, holding a hand across her stomach. "At least I am, I hope he is."

Hannah discreetly wiped her eye and held her arms out for her son. "Did you have fun?"

EJ went into her arms, hugging her tightly. God, she'd needed that hug, but she wished desperately it had been his dad giving it to her. She tried her best to listen as he babbled on about what he and Shell had done at the park, but she realized for the first time in a while he'd gotten taller. The dimple in his cheek was deepening, and he was losing a lot of the baby fat he'd had. He was becoming more and more like Garrett every day, and Garrett was missing it.

Her heart broke.

They were all missing out on so much.

"Han, what's wrong?" Shell asked, alarm in her voice.

Hannah realized tears were streaming down her face. When Shell removed EJ from her hold and called for one of the band members EJ was comfortable with, she didn't try and hold him to her. Instead, she folded in on herself, trying to keep the sobs as quiet as possible.

"This is all wrong." She shook her head, holding her hand across her stomach.

"*What's* wrong? Talk to me."

How did she tell another woman the things running through her head? She knew she was setting feminism back years, but it was her personal choice.

"Being here without Garrett, doing this without him at my side. I can't do it. This has to be the end of it, at least until EJ and whatever kids we may have in the future are old enough to be on their own." She toyed with her wedding ring. "I'm not strong enough, and he's missing out on so much, but if EJ were with him, I'd be missing out. It's not fair." She shook her head.

"Honey." Shell grabbed her around the neck and pulled her close. "You love your career and you love your family."

"But something is going to have to give," she argued. "And you know I'm right. We can't both have what we want. It's easier for me to give up a part of what I'm doing than it is for him."

"You've said this before, Han. Are you serious this time?"

Faced with having her family versus not having her family, she knew she was as serious as she'd ever been.

"I am. This is it."

Chapter Twenty-Eight

H annah stood outside the tour bus Shell and Jared had ridden on together, EJ in her arms as she knocked on the door. Today they had most of the day free, and she'd planned an excursion to a play center with EJ. Since she figured Shell was missing Jared as much as she was Garrett, she had decided to ask her to come with them.

"Yeah." Shell answered the door, her face red.

"You okay?" Hannah hadn't seen her friend this upset since the guys had left.

"I just miss him today, ya know?"

Hannah did know; it was one of the reasons she was making it a point to get out and about. "Well, EJ and I have a fun-filled day planned, and he wanted to know if Aunt Shell wanted to come with us."

Shell looked for a few seconds like she wanted to say no, then she rethought the idea. "You know what? I'd love to. When are you leaving?"

"I have to change." She indicated the workout clothes she was wearing. "Get him changed, and pack his bag. Thirty minutes to an hour?"

"Sounds good to me."

As Hannah walked over to her tour bus, she pulled her phone out of her pocket and pulled up Jared's number, composing a quick text.

Call your wife. She misses you.

Shell tried to get hold of her emotions as she went to the back of the tour bus she and Jared had shared while he was on tour with them. His being gone was hard for her and was one of the reasons she'd taken to spending more time on Hannah's tour bus. Everywhere on this bus were reminders of Jared.

Instead, she spent most of her time working, and what time she wasn't working, she usually switched busses. Today, though, she was going to get out with Hannah and EJ if it killed her.

Just as she started putting her hair up, she saw a FaceTime request from Jared. She'd missed his last one, so she grabbed hold of this one with both hands and had a seat.

"Hey." She did her best to smile happily for him, but the smile fell when she saw the worried look on his face.

"Hey," he answered back. "I miss you."

The first words always out of his mouth. God, she missed him too, everything about him, and right now she hated his record label with everything she had. "I miss you too." As she said the words her face crumbled and she gave into the tears.

"Sweetheart, don't do this to me." He got up from where he was sitting and she could hear him walking down a hallway, and then they were in a room alone. "God, you're killing me."

"I'm sorry." She sniffed. "I'm so sorry, but I'm not used to this anymore. I'm not used to being without you. You always say I'm your rock, but J, you're mine, and I'm lost right now."

"Wipe your eyes, please. I can't see you cry." He grasped his lip ring between his teeth, pulling on it.

He always did that when he was pensive, when he had too many thoughts running through his head.

"This sucks." She breathed out deeply. "Like every part of it sucks, every single part of it. I love you and I wanna be with you, but Hannah's my best friend and I love her too."

"There's no decision to be made here," he assured her. "I know right now this feels bigger than the both of us, but it's pretty simple, Shell. I miss you, you miss me, and eventually this will work out so we can be together full-time."

"I hope so." She bit her bottom lip. "I got way too used to having you around."

"Gorgeous, I wake up every morning reaching for you. Don't think for five seconds that this has been easy on me, or that I wouldn't change our situation in a heartbeat if I could."

At least they were on the same page. She wiped her eyes, breathing deeply again. "I'm going with Hannah and EJ this afternoon. We're getting out and about. She hasn't had a lot of time to spend with him, and frankly, I think we're sick of being sad."

"Good, I want you to. What are you doing?"

"Something about a play center. If it's like the last one we took him to, it's got slides and foam pits, and all kinds of fun stuff. He loves it, and to be honest, I kinda do too." She laughed, letting a smile shine through.

"Keep doing that." He grinned back at her. "Please keep smiling. If I know you're not, it breaks my heart."

"I'll try." She tilted her to the side and scrunched her nose. "It's the most I can promise you right now."

"Then I'll take it."

There was a knock at the door, and he glanced at the watch on his wrist. "I gotta go, but promise me you'll have a good time today, and don't forget to call me tonight. I know you've not been calling because it's harder for you to hear my voice and then know I'm not gonna be there. But I need you as much as you need me."

"I love you." She blew a kiss into the phone. "And I'll definitely remember that you wait for me as much as I wait for you."

They disconnected, and she felt lighter than she had in days, but she still couldn't wait until they could be together again.

"Lord, my legs hurt." Hannah laughed as she watched Shell coming down the slide with EJ in her lap.

They'd climbed up and down the slide what felt like a

million times, and Hannah had never been so happy she'd brought someone with her.

"Again!" EJ grabbed his mom's hand and started pulling her up the stairs.

"One more time," she told him. "Then we have to go because mama's gotta go to work."

"I'll just sit down here and try to remember I'm not twenty-one anymore." Shell breathed heavily as she walked over to a bench and took a load off.

"This is so going to hurt in the morning," Hannah yelled back at her.

"It already hurts," Shell answered.

It had been a long day, but Hannah was glad she'd gotten to spend some time with EJ. The only thing was she wished Garrett was there with them. He'd been looking for his dad all day, but he'd not made a scene, and for that she was happy. It was hard enough doing things on her own without having him break down when he realized Garrett wasn't there.

"Are you ready?" she asked him as they had a seat on the slide. "This is the last time so let's make it count."

EJ held his hands up and squealed as she pushed them off, and they went flying down the inflatable slide. She had to admit, it was one of the more fun things they'd ever done. As they came to the bottom, Shell stood and took a picture of them.

"Here, you should send this to Garrett and let him know all the fun he missed."

When she got the picture from Shell, she did that, but didn't tell him about the fun he missed. She let him know how missed he was.

*Had fun today, but we really missed you. Smiles hide
a lot of loneliness.*

She texted the picture to him before she put her
phone in her back pocket and went about getting their
shoes and paying for their fun day.

When they got out to the car they were using for the
day, she had a text back from Garrett.

*Babe, you're killing me. There's nothing I wouldn't do
to be there with you two right now. I hope you know
that.*

She knew he would with everything she had in her.

I know, believe me I know.

After strapping EJ in, she felt her phone vibrate
again, and she checked the message, seeing a picture
from the photo shoot they'd had for the album. It was
the one Garret had made his lock screen the minute the
picture had been texted to them.

This is the only thing getting me through right now.

She fought back tears, but told herself she wouldn't
be melancholy, not today.

*It gets me through too. Just remember, Garrett. To-
gether we're strong, so if you've got me, I've got you.*

Chapter Twenty-Nine

"Thanks for coming to pick us up." Hannah held a sleeping EJ on her hip as she, Shell, and Stacey made their way through LAX.

"Not a problem, although I think you highly under-estimated the amount of paparazzi being here at night once they heard you were coming."

Hannah's heart dropped as she saw the waiting throng of photographers. She never wanted to expose EJ to things like this, at least not until he was old enough to know what was going on. She worried he would be scared, but she knew they had to get through this madness to get to Garrett. Squaring her shoulders, she grabbed EJ tighter, and the three of them tried to make their way through.

"Harmony, how does it feel to be back on the West Coast? Have you missed Reaper?"

They were creeping in. "Please move," she begged. EJ was starting to wake up. When he fully realized what was going on she could tell, because he tensed and let out an awful wail.

"Please move back," she yelled louder this time.

"It's okay," she tried to soothe EJ who screamed in her ear.

"He's scared! Please move back! I'll answer any questions you have, but please give us some room."

Shell was attempting to be her muscle as she tried to push the huge amount of people back. Keeping her head down, Hannah kept walking, hoping at some point they would get to a spot where they could make a break for it. EJ screamed and clung to her. It was at that point she told herself she'd never do this again. She'd never subject her child to being without his family again. If Garrett had been with them, this wouldn't be happening right now.

"I brought back up. He's just got to get to us," Stacey was saying over the ruckus.

It was then she heard a loud male voice tell everyone to back up, and EJ reached out, yelling, *"Papa!"* Her father-in-law to the rescue. She could have cried as she felt Kevin's big hands wrap around EJ and take him from her arms. It made it much easier for the group of them to get through the melee. Security arrived just in time too, allowing her to finally have some breathing room.

"Thanks for coming to the rescue again." She smiled up at the guy who could be Garrett's older brother as she wiped away the tear tracks on EJ's face.

"I would have been there sooner, but I had to park the car. It's so good to see all of you."

She took a deep breath, smelling the difference between Tennessee and California. Both were familiar to her, but Tennessee would always be home. When they approached what they saw was both Stacey and Kevin's cars, Shell and Hannah glanced around.

"I'm taking you two to the studio, and dad's taking EJ for the night."

Hannah's heart sped up as she thought about what that meant – a night alone with just her husband. EJ would be taken care of. She'd left Havock back on the tour bus, and they would be completely and entirely alone.

"You can come get him in the morning, or whatever, but we've missed the little guy, and he needs time with us too."

Understanding completely what he was saying, she reached over, kissing EJ on the cheek. "Be good for Mimi and Papa?"

He nodded, his eyes already starting to close. He was so tired, and she knew all he wanted was a bed to sleep in too. "I love you." She pushed his hair back from his forehead. She laughed as he waved tiredly at her. They helped Kevin get EJ strapped in, and they all said their goodbye' before Hannah turned to Stacey. An idea was forming in her brain, one she couldn't wait to put into motion. "If you don't care, take me home, I'd rather not go to the studio."

Garrett couldn't concentrate as he kept checking the time on his phone. He knew Stacey and his dad had been going to pick up the girls and EJ, but he figured they should be close by now. His hands itched to touch her, his lips wanted to capture hers, and his cock was ready to spend hours getting reacquainted with her.

They were putting the final touches on the song they were working on when the door opened, and Jared hopped up from his seat. "I fucking missed you," they could hear him say as he grabbed Shell up in his arms.

Garrett glanced behind Shell and Stacey. "Where's my wife?"

Stacey gave him a wink. "She had us take her home."

"Then I'm out. See you all later."

He grabbed his stuff and all but ran out the door. As he got to his SUV, a text message popped on his phone. It was a media message; he clicked the download button, and as he pulled himself into the driver's seat, a moan ripped from his throat. It was Hannah, with a shot that obscured her face, pulling her shirt part of the way down over her chest. There was nothing indecent, but it was the tease he loved.

You know how you always get to be Reaper with me?
Tonight I get to be Harmony with you.

The text caught his attention, and he blew through every traffic law he knew getting home to her.

Garrett wasn't sure where she would be as he pulled into the garage and turned the car off. His body was humming with need. It felt like years since he'd seen her—FaceTime and text weren't the same as having her with him all the time. They'd known it would be difficult, but it was as if he'd forgotten how hard those early days of their relationship had been. Now with EJ, it'd been even worse. He'd seen a picture she'd posted on Instagram the other day and almost cried because of how different he looked. His son was growing up without him there.

Getting out, he went inside, calling out her name as he made it to the kitchen and through the living room. When he didn't see her around, he decided to check the bedroom. Taking the stairs two at a time, he tried to calm down his racing heart. He felt like he was about to come out of his skin. His fingers needed to touch her, though. He needed to smell her shampoo, her perfume; he needed to fucking gorge on her mouth and her body. The bedroom door was open, and when he stepped over the threshold, he didn't expect to see her sitting on the bed all demure with her legs crossed.

"Hey, handsome." She grinned, not getting up.

She had on stage makeup, and her hair was done much like it was on stage, but he could tell she'd probably had a shower before they'd gotten on the plane. She wore a dress she sometimes brought out for one of the slower numbers that he always teased her about. It had a low-cut neckline that framed her tits perfectly, along with a short skirt that showed off the leg muscles she'd gotten from running around after EJ.

"Hey, Harmony." He smiled back at her.

It felt foreign to call her that name, but her eyes lit with recognition when he did. He was down for whatever game she wanted to play. Tonight they were whatever they wanted to be to one another. They weren't parents or multi-platinum artists with millions of followers and fans, tonight they were Reaper and Harmony, and he had a feeling things were about to get hot.

"You got my text, huh?"

He palmed the cock that jutted against the zipper of his pants. "I did, and I have the hard-on to prove it."

Her gaze traveled down to where he gripped himself. Pushing her tongue against her teeth, she licked her lips like she was ready for a treat.

"The question is what are you going to do with me?"

It wasn't in him to give up complete control to her, but he was willing to let her play. He watched as she stood up from where she sat on the bed, sauntering over to him in those fuck-me heels she liked to wear sometimes.

"That's a good question. *What* am I going to do with you?"

He followed her as she made a circle around his body, touching him here and there, running her hand down his chest, stopping at the belt of his buckle. He watched as she got rid of it with sure hands and pushed the pants down his legs.

"I'll tell you what I want." Her voice was seductive as she stood directly in front of him, so close he could feel her breath on his chin.

"What's that?"

"You to completely strip and lie down on the bed. Think you can do that?"

His eyes meeting her, he nodded that he could before performing the task she'd asked. Completely naked,
trying to ignore the hard pole at his midsection, he lay
down, waiting for her to make her next move.

Chapter Thirty

Hannah watched as Garrett lay flat on his back, motioning for her with a raise of his eyebrow. She hadn't been sure what she wanted to do when he walked in, but she had an idea now. He looked delectable lying there for her. Garrett had always been a good-looking guy, and he never failed to turn her on, but tonight he had stubble, his hair was unkempt, and there were dark circles under his eyes. It gave him the look of someone who was dark and dangerous. It made her wet.

Slipping her heels off, she walked over to the bed and climbed on, using her knees to walk over to where he lay.

"I'm yours to do what you want." He gestured down his body.

Hannah let her eyes roam, coming to stop at the hard cock jutting out from a neatly trimmed thatch of hair. There were many things she wanted tonight, and she wasn't at all positive she could voice them all, but she would try. "I want to see what you do when I'm not around. How do you make the tension go away?"

His eyes burned dark and with an electricity she'd never seen. He looked as if he wasn't sure what she was asking, but when his big hand enclosed his thick length, she knew he understood.

"It doesn't feel as good as when you do it." His voice was thick with arousal, the sound of him jerking up and down loud in the room.

"Nothing ever feels as good as it does when we're together," she assured him.

With wide eyes, she watched for a few moments, her eyes riveted on his face. He sucked his bottom lip in between his teeth, tilting his head back as he used the edge of his palm to cover the tip of his erection.

She wasn't sure she could do what was running through her head, but she knew she had to try. "I know what I want." She cleared her throat.

"Oh, babe, tell me." His eyes met hers, and it wasn't her imagination that he sped up his pace.

Hiking the dress up over her thighs, she showed him she wore no panties. A bra wasn't practical with the low-cut of the dress, so save for the fabric that covered her; nothing separated her skin from his. She carefully straddled his chest, letting her moist core rub up and down his sternum. She moaned, trailing her hand up her waist, over one of her breasts and through her hair, letting her fingertips fall back to her chest. Carefully, she pulled one side of the dress down, taking out her bare breast, before using the tip of her finger to manipulate and tease her pebbled nipple.

"Waiting here, Harmony," Garrett reminded her.

Shaking her head, she knocked herself out of her trance-like state. She wasn't sure she could say the words, but she was so hot, and she needed him so much. "I want your tongue on me, I want your mouth on me, and I wanna come that way."

"You want to ride my face?" His eyebrows were up in his hairline, and his hand stopped on his dick.

Her face flashed hot, and she was worried he'd say no, but she went for it anyway. "Yeah, that's exactly what I want. I got bored one night, and found something on the internet, I wanna try it," she broke off.

"Oh *fuck yeah*." Garrett breathed deeply through his nose. "This will be my pleasure. I can't fuckin' believe you told me you want to do this."

She couldn't either, but Harmony had way more guts than Hannah ever would.

Hannah felt stupid situated where she was, but Garrett assured her she would love it. Spreading her legs, she lowered herself until she felt the tip of his tongue on the place that needed him the most.

"Ohhhh," she moaned, lowering a bit further.

He grasped her thighs, pulling her so far down she was afraid she'd suffocate him, but then he swiped against her swollen arousal with his tongue, and she was done. Reaching out, she grasped the headboard with one hand, her loose hanging tit with the other, and gave her body over to the feelings coursing through it.

"Oh my God." She breathed, her mouth forming an

"O" as she panted, rotating her hips against his invasion.

Her head fell forward on her shoulders and she glanced down, seeing Garrett's eyes. They were so hot, so dark, so on fire for her, and it was more than she could take. He moved his hands so that they bracketed her thighs, pulling them further apart as he positively lapped up every bit of moisture flowing from her body. She couldn't stop her hips from rotating, couldn't stop her pussy from thrusting towards him, and she knew she didn't want to stop.

The feelings he evoked in her were of another world. She'd never felt anything as strong as this, not from any of the encounters they'd ever had before. She swore to herself each time he made love to her, each time he took her, each time he even kissed her, it was better than the last, but dear God, this one was blowing them all out of the water.

She was pushing for the orgasm, straining against his ministrations, wanting the feeling of euphoria that lay just out of reach. Using both hands, she grasped the headboard so hard her fingers hurt, but it was the only way she could deal with the feeling of his tongue making contact with her clit.

"That feels so good." She panted. "So good, don't stop, don't stop, don't stop…" The plea was a litany as she ground against him.

Her eyes popped open when he grabbed hold of her clit with his lips and then used his tongue to stimulate the nub the same way he did with her nipple, and she couldn't stop the nonsense that fell out of her mouth.

"Oh my God, Garrett, so good, so good, please don't stop." She let her head fall forward again, this time making contact with the headboard as she rode out the waves of pleasure. "So horny, I've needed you so bad, so bad," she kept speaking, not even sure she was making sense. "So many nights, I've just wanted you to fuck me," she continued, amazed at herself.

He moaned loudly himself when she told him she'd wanted him to fuck her. After those words fell from her lips, he seemed to have a one-track mind, and then she felt one of his hands leave her thigh. When she heard the tell-tale slap of skin against skin, she realized he was masturbating as he was getting her off.

The knowledge he was servicing himself while servicing her was the most erotic thing she'd ever known in her life. His other hand left the other thigh and went straight to her pussy, holding the lips apart while he moved his tongue double time.

Surrounded by the erotic sounds, her body was on a one-way track to coming. And when it did, she wasn't prepared for it.

"Oh *fuck*," she screamed, her hips canting against Garrett's face, her clit brushing his nose. "Oh my God, oh shit." She couldn't stop her hips from moving, even as she felt her body letting go as the tremors moved through her thighs. Tears fell and she didn't know why, but the release was that powerful, and just as she went to move off Garrett's face, she heard something from him that made her come again, without even being touched.

"Harmony, shit, didn't even have to touch me and

I'm coming." He groaned, his hand jacking his cock so fast the bed bounced.

She felt the evidence against her exposed butt, and more aftershocks ran through her body as he continued to move his hand along his length, cursing again.

"Mother fuck, I can't stop coming." He inhaled deeply and she felt the evidence again.

Finally their two bodies stopped moving against each other, and they seemed to calm down slightly.

"Holy shit, that's never happened before." Garrett ran his hand up and down her back, his voice hoarse.

Hers was too; she hadn't screamed that loudly in a long time. She knew he was talking about coming so many times so quickly together. "Same here." She buried her head in his shoulder, bashful but proud.

"Goddamn." He kissed her neck. "That's proof we don't need to be apart that long again."

She completely agreed with him. "That's why after this tour is over; I'm done until EJ and whatever future children we have are of age."

"Are you sure?" he asked, pulling back so they could look at each other.

"Yeah, it's for the best. Not just for us, but for Shell and Jared too. They can't stand this anymore than we can."

They were quiet as they enjoyed each other's company for the first time in weeks.

Chapter Thirty-One

The next morning, well-rested and with the tension the two of them had been carrying gone, they picked up their son and brought him home, choosing to spend the day together.

"Shut the front door," Hannah yelled as she glanced at her phone.

"What?" he asked as he slipped into the driver's seat after buckling EJ in.

"My new single just hit number one on the pop charts." She flipped her phone around and showed him the message, along with the chart to reference.

"Babe! That's amazing."

There was something about the way he said it; his excitement didn't quite meet his eyes.

"What's wrong?" she asked as they backed out of the driveway.

"Does this change what you said last night? I mean a pop number one is a huge accomplishment that not even some pop stars ever get. You're a country star and you've done it. This means huge things for you."

Her answer was straight and to the point, much like it had been the night before. "Nothing changes how I feel about what's right for my family. Garrett, money and fame is all good, but what matters to me is waking up next to you every morning and walking down the hallway with Havock at my feet, going to get EJ. My priorities and dreams have changed. Will they change again? Maybe. We all grow. But right now, I need to be with my family. If this is meant to be for me, it'll still be here when we're ready for it."

He reached over, grasping her hand in his before bringing her knuckles up to his lips, brushing a kiss along the skin there. "I'll support you no matter what."

"You've already done that, more times than I deserve, but right now it's time for me to be with my family."

"Then let's get home and enjoy the time we have together before you have to leave again."

"How about this?" Garrett grabbed EJ from where he stood between them on the kitchen floor. "I'll do the dishes, you start dinner, and we'll put up the baby gate so he's confined to this room with us. We'll get double the stuff done in half the time."

"Great idea." Hannah gave a huge sigh of relief as she watched Garrett immediately start putting the baby gates up on either side of the room. She smiled when he grabbed a handful of toys amongst EJ's favorites and dropped them in the middle of the floor.

"Here ya go, little man."

EJ loved to be in the same room as them and loved when he thought he was part of the action. He gave them a toothy grin as he plopped down and began immediately playing with the toy that made the most noise.

Garrett laughed. "Go ahead, bang it out."

Hannah laughed along with him. "Anything to make a bunch of noise, he's all for."

She walked over to the fridge, grabbing out the vegetables and hamburger meat she would need before leaning up into the pantry to grab taco seasoning and their favorite tortilla chips. Nachos were a Thompson family staple. Reaching into the bottom cupboard, she got her skillet and got the hamburger going.

"I always get water all over myself when I do this," Garrett grumbled.

Glancing over, Hannah laughed loudly when he turned around; bubbles up to his elbows and water all down the front of his shirt. "You are so messy." She laughed. "You wanna just take it off?"

He gave her a wink when her hands went to the hem of his T-shirt. "Strip me, please."

"Stop." She giggled, pushing the T-shirt he wore up and over his head before throwing it over the baby gate into the living room. Regardless of how hot he looked today with his messy hair, unshaven face, and sleepy eyes, she hadn't meant anything by taking his shirt off. "There was nothing sexual about it."

"Not from where I stand, babe. Anytime you take

my clothes off, I'm ready to go."

Rolling her eyes and grinning, she turned back to her skillet, turning the heat down as her food had started cooking faster than she wanted it to. On the floor, EJ banged loudly on his toy, laughing when the two of them stopped what they were doing, giving him their attention.

"You want some music?" Garrett asked. They had Bluetooth speakers in most of the rooms.

"Oh, that's a good idea!"

Going over to the counter, she grabbed his cell phone and went to his Spotify. He used it for everything—working out, driving, whatever the case may be. She knew she'd find a huge amount of variety on the workout playlist though. Scrolling through the songs, she found one, her smile huge.

"Oh my God, I can't believe you have this song on here." She laughed, almost snorting.

"If it's my workout playlist, there's no telling what it is." He made no apologies as he finished with the dishes and grabbed a towel to take care of his hands.

Mind made up, Hannah pressed play, laughing when they heard *This Is How We Do It* over the speakers.

"Oh my God." He threw his head straight back against his shoulders, laughing so hard she could see his ab muscles flex against his skin.

As soon as the music started, he danced over to her. Her giggles echoed off the cabinets. "If people could see Reaper now," she teased as he reached out, grabbed her hands, and spun her around the kitchen.

"C'mon, I know you can shake your ass." He

mouthed the words of the song to her as they got into a dance off. On the floor EJ clapped his hands loudly for both of them. "See, even he knows it."

Turning so that her back was to him, she looked over her shoulder and did just as he'd asked, shaking her hips as she sang along. She'd never seen him pulling some of the moves, but Garrett had rhythm. She let him put his hands on her hips, getting all into her personal space, dipping his head down against her neck. She smiled back at him, grabbing hold of EJ who'd stood up in front of them, wanting to get in on the action.

Her hands moved EJ's arms up and down as his feet stomped, completely in tune with the music. He was a complete natural. As the music wound down, Garrett clapped his hands for EJ, who beamed under the praise. It was only then they heard loud clapping that wasn't their own that they turned around.

"Y'all that was the cutest thing I think I've ever seen in my life. Next time you might wanna make sure the door's locked or you're not listening to the music so loud." Shell stood in front of them, her cell phone at the ready.

"Did you video our dancing?" Garrett asked.

"Is that what your flailing around was?" she questioned him, knowing it would get under his skin. "I sure did." She laughed as she pressed some buttons on her phone. "And it's now on Harmony's Instagram. Oh I can't wait to see the comments about this."

"You are so dead," Garrett vowed as he took off towards her, vaulting over the baby gate as she squealed, making for the front door.

Hannah shook her head as she finished cooking the food. Never a dull moment in the Thompson household.

Chapter Thirty-Two

"This is it, babe, last concert of the tour." She'd know Garrett's voice anywhere, but she was giddy to hear it tonight.

It'd been four weeks since they'd last seen each other in California, and it wasn't like those weeks had passed with the snap of her fingers. They'd had more arguments than she'd cared to count, at one point EJ had quit talking to her, and for a couple of days Havock had stopped eating. Tonight, though, marked the end of this period in her life. She'd spoken with the record company and explained her position.

They hadn't exactly been welcoming to the fact she wanted to quit and form her own record label, but they'd at least understood why she needed to do it. Tonight was her final show, and afterward, Garrett would be taking them to Hawaii before he finished recording and then Black Friday would be announcing their own tour. They'd gone to Hawaii one Christmas before and it had been her favorite place to vacation since.

"I know." She laughed. "What are you going to do

about me being with you twenty-four/seven? You'll get sick of me after a while."

"I don't think that's possible. We did it once already, not too long ago, ya know?"

God, it seemed like forever ago when she'd sat in the car and told him she was ready to go back into the studio. It literally felt like years when it'd only been months. It wasn't like she'd forgotten how quickly things worked in this industry, but she had truly forgotten how quickly things got old. And that's where she was now, completely done with this part of her life.

"Will you be okay that I'm a washed-up has been at twenty-eight?" She leaned up, kissing him on the cheek.

"You crazy? That means I have a sexy-ass stay-at-home wife who will be there to service me whenever I need it. And you're young enough to still have that smoking body." He played along with her.

She loved him for everything he was able to do for her. For all the ways he took her mind off the crap that continued to find doubts in her everyday life—for the way he loved her, no matter what her damage was. She'd found a once in a lifetime love with Garrett Thompson, and she knew no amount of wanting to be on stage would ever take the place of what they had together. It was a simple as that.

"You ready?" he asked her as she shook her hair free of the curlers she'd been wearing.

"Yeah," she admitted. "I'm tired, and I wanna be with you. I don't want to sleep apart anymore; I don't want to wake up without you by my side. I just want us back."

He wrapped her up in his arms, kissing her forehead. "I want us back too, babe, but remember what I've always said. I don't want the *us* to be at the expense of you."

She'd never forget those words because they'd been the sweetest he'd ever spoken.

"San Diego!" She waved to the crowd they were playing for tonight. "It feels so good to be saying goodbye to the tour here tonight."

The crowd screamed, appreciative of the show she'd been putting on for them. The last time she'd done a last concert of the tour, it'd been bittersweet. She'd taken everything in and hadn't wanted it to end. Tonight, she was doing her best to slow herself down, not to rush it so the fans could get the type of show they'd paid for.

"Do you all mind if I bring my husband out on stage? He's taking me on vacation after the show tonight." She grinned at them, listening as she got a resounding yes.

Again, Garrett came on stage, wearing his Harmony Stewart shirt. It never failed to make her laugh, and she knew part of the reason he wore it was to make her laugh. As he sat down and Jared and Shell joined them, she realized she did want to look back on *this* memory and live in it. This was what meant the most. Good friends, good music, and good fun.

"Your letter to your followers will post in about thirty

minutes," Shell told her as they got ready to go their separate ways. Jared was taking her for a trip someplace where none of them could talk about work. "Other than that, I'll see you in five days."

They hugged, each wishing the other a great time.

"Give mama a hug," Garrett told EJ as he passed his son over to Hannah. They were leaving EJ with his West Coast family for the week. At first they'd wanted to take him on their Hawaii getaway, but everyone had rallied around and told them they needed time to themselves. In the end, they'd relented.

She hugged him tightly, kissing him on the forehead, telling him to be good and she would FaceTime him whenever possible, before she handed him over to Marie. "It's like he doesn't even care." She laughed.

Marie gave her a sympathetic look. "Kids are resilient. Call whenever you need to, but have fun with your husband."

That had been the phrase everyone had told her, so she definitely planned to.

She and Garrett held hands as they waved to family and friends before making their way into the airport and to their terminal.

"You worried about the letter you wrote?"

She shook her head. "I meant every word of it, and like everyone always tells me, if they're true fans, they'll get it."

I wanted to take a second and let you all know what's going on. I know some of you have heard whispers and tabloids have been talking about my leaving country music to go pop since I've had two number ones there this year.

Well, they're right, and they're wrong.

I'm leaving, but it's not country music. It's all music for right now.

If there's one thing I learned on this tour and in the past few months, it's that I'm not cut out to be a working mother. I'm not cut out to let my husband be halfway across the country from me and let him see his child grow up through pictures.

This business isn't easy and neither is marriage.

When you put the two together, you're never sure what's going to come out at the end.

Me, I choose my marriage. I choose my family.

I hope you'll understand. I'm still going to record, but there won't be any touring until EJ and any future children are of age. I'll be active here like I've always been, and I'll be on stage with Reaper like I've always been. It might be selfish, but my family comes first.

I love the job, I love y'all, but I also love a two-year-old with dimples who calls me mom and a green-eyed hunk of a man that worships the ground I walk on.

I'd be stupid to give it up, and I hope that you all understand.

Love,
Harmony

Hannah got the notification her post had gone live and then shut her phone off. She wasn't interested in hearing what anyone who wasn't in her life had to say. This was her decision and she was sticking to it.

Chapter Thirty-Three

"They aren't kidding when they say this place was paradise." Garrett took a drink of his beer, stretching out on the lanai of their hotel room.

Hannah glanced over from where she lay next to him, drinking her own fruity concoction. "No they weren't. I could get used to this, and to be honest, I'm kind of scared to go back to reality in two days. I feel like we should just have your mom and dad fly EJ here and buy a house on the beach."

He laughed. "Havock would love it at least. I think he's had enough of Tennessee. Sometimes I see him gazing out at the grass, and I think I hear him wishing for the ocean."

She laughed, throwing a hand against him stomach. "Stop, he loves where we live. Actually he loves being anywhere EJ is."

"He does," Garrett agreed, pushing his sunglasses down further on his face. He'd been dozing off and on for the past hour. He was still tired from the parasailing excursion they'd done yesterday. It had been totally worth it, but a day on the ocean had drained him.

"Do you think he'd be that way about any kids we have?" she asked quietly.

"Hannah?" he questioned.

"No I'm not pregnant." She held up her drink. "Would I be drinking if I was pregnant? But I will be honest with you and tell you it's crossed my mind lately. Would it be so bad to add another kid to the mix? I've always wanted two, and with EJ being two, now would be the perfect time to try."

She said it all in a rush, and Garrett could tell she'd probably been thinking on it for a long time.

"I'm up to the challenge if you are," he told her honestly. He'd do anything with her, as long as they were together and worked as a team. Being married wasn't hard with her, their relationship came easy, and while sometimes they argued, he knew they were pretty damn solid.

"Really?" Her eyes held a look of anticipation, and it made him happy he'd been the one to put it there.

"Seriously, if it's something you want to do, when we get home, go to the doctor, get off the birth control, and we'll let nature take its course. I love our family, and I'd be excited to add another kid into the mix. Maybe this time we could have a little girl with your smile and your eyes. That'd make me happier than anything in the world."

"I didn't think you'd agree to it," she admitted as she took a sip of her drink.

"It's not to say I'm not a little nervous. You were so

sick before, and leaving you when you had to tour was the absolute hardest thing in the world. I felt like such a piece of shit, and the worst husband to walk the face of the earth. Maybe that's something we can talk to the doctor about, get it straightened out before it starts." He took a drink of his beer. "Besides, have I ever told you no about something you really wanted?" He pursed his lips at her, shooting her a bored look.

"That house on the beach here, you didn't seem receptive to the idea." She squealed when he reached over and pulled her into his lap.

Lifting the hair off the nape of her neck, he pulled her into a kiss. "How about we practice for when we get our shot? I wanna make sure we get it on the first try like we did last time."

Her body heated up at the thought. "Sounds like a good way to spend the afternoon to me."

Hours later, they lay in bed still kissing. They'd spent the afternoon with him inside her, and even now as he lay between her spread legs, leaning his head down to capture one bare nipple between his teeth.

"I don't think I can ever get enough of you." He rubbed his cheek against the nub, teasing it with the stubble he was sporting.

"I hope you never do." She wound her fingers through his hair, pulling his mouth back to where he had been teasing. "Again?" She smiled sleepily at him.

God, he wasn't sure he could come again, but there

no mistaking the thick length of his erection against her thigh. He couldn't believe he was hard again. Not after having her three times since they'd come inside. The lanai door was open and a soft rain had begun to fall at some point during their afternoon of love, and it caused a chill in the air.

Using his left hand, he pulled the sheet down to expose her other breast to his gaze, cupping it as the tip pulled taught against the coolness of the room.

"I love looking down and seeing your wedding ring." She pushed her feet against the mattress, pressing up into him, giving herself over to the desire running through them.

She was wet, having already taken three of his releases, and it helped him slide past the swollen flesh that greeted him. "I love yours too." He leaned down, nipping at her collarbone. "That little piece of jewelry that says you belong to me always gets me hot." He nosed into her neck, capturing her pulse point with his lips.

They were quiet as they continued to push and pull against each other. It wasn't the pulse-pounding coming together it normally was for them; this was lazy, dream inducing, and full of the type of eroticism normally found in soft porn.

When they came, it was quiet, understated, and slow.

Garrett lifted his head from Hannah's breast. "I think I'm done for." His face was sleepy, his eyes heavy, his tone the most relaxed she'd ever heard it.

Grasping him around the neck, she answered with a

yawn. "I think I am too."

With the quiet of the raining Hawaii afternoon around them, they fell into the sleep of two lovers who'd worn each other out and had nothing but time together on their schedule.

Chapter Thirty-Four

Five Months Later

Hannah grinned as she stood in the back of the room as the record label and Black Friday make a huge announcement. They would be holding one of the biggest rock shows ever in the US, the first one that would rival the rock festivals in Europe, and her husband's band was headlining. More than likely this would catapult them into the stratosphere, and she couldn't wait. They were some of the hardest working guys and *the* hardest working band she'd ever met.

"Shhh, Daddy's talking." She did her best to shush EJ as she listened to Garrett.

"We're really excited to introduce the US to the kind of show that's been taking place overseas and in South America for years. For one place here in the states to hold sixty-thousand-fans strong…we're beyond excited. To headline that show? It's an amazing honor, and one we feel privileged to accept."

Hannah's heart exploded with pride as she watched the guys handle the press as seasoned veterans. It was time for the people at home to see just how polished her guys were.

"You doing okay?" Shell asked as she stood with them and bent to grab for EJ. He went willingly up into her arms, scampering until he could put his arms around her.

Hannah rubbed her stomach, smiling ruefully as she looked at her son. Hard to believe he'd be three this year and would soon be a big brother.

"C'mon, Havock," she argued with the dog. "Let me get this shirt on you."

He looked at her like he wanted to go pee on the carpet and then let it sit there for a few hours before alerting anyone to it.

"You'll have another baby." She pitched her voice in the tone he liked. "You know how you take care of EJ and you two love each other? You'll have another one."

Finally she got him to let her put his paws through the arm-holes of the shirt. Breathing heavily, she sat back on her knees, admiring her handiwork. Both EJ and Havock wore shirts proclaiming they were going to be big brothers.

It had taken much longer than she'd thought it would, and she started to panic when she heard the garage door opening.

"EJ, c'mere!"

He came running in, and she scooped him up right as Garrett came through the back door. Immediately, his eyes took in what was before him.

"Big Brother? Are you sure?" He had a huge grin on his face.

"Found out for sure today!"

He sat his stuff on the counter and grabbed both her and EJ in his arms. "I wondered, but you weren't sick."

"I know." She laughed loudly. "I wasn't sure myself, but we confirmed it today. We're now a two-child family."

And she couldn't have been happier.

They were doing their best to keep this second pregnancy under wraps, and so far, ten weeks in, she hadn't been plagued by the same sickness that had rendered her useless last time. The only she thing she needed was a power nap early in the afternoon and an early bedtime. She hoped even that would go away as the pregnancy wore on.

"I feel like I should be an old hand at this. I was pregnant when they toured last time," she smirked.

The press conference concluded, and she waited patiently for Garrett to get done before he walked over to them. Their eyes caught as he glanced up from the person he was talking to. Didn't matter how long they'd been together, how many arguments they had, or how many issues they lived through, she knew there would always be this magnetic attraction that ran through the both of them.

"Good God." Shell sighed. "If you weren't already pregnant, you'd *be* pregnant by the time he stopped eating you up with his eyes."

She didn't mind at all. He took EJ from Shell's arms, holding him tightly to his chest before bending down and placing a chaste kiss on Hannah's lips. "How are you?"

"Hungry," she admitted, grasping hold of his hand as

he reached down to caress the stomach that didn't yet have a bump.

"Then let's get outta here, we can't have you hungry."

She loved the possessive look in his eyes, the way his body shielded hers as they walked towards their vehicle, and the sure way he held their son in his arms. Without a doubt he would do the same for the child they were going to have in a few months' time, and she knew she'd fall even more in love with him. He opened the door for her, ushering her into the SUV before walking back to put their son in his car seat.

Glancing out at the Nashville skyline, she watched as the sun started to set, a content smile on her face. Over the years many people had tried to tell her who to be, what to feel, and how to behave. Instead she felt at peace with the decisions she'd made that led her to this quiet afternoon, because no matter what hat she wore or what role she played—above all she was most comfortable with her friends and family.

Epilogue

Hannah Thompson grasped her son, EJ, around the waist as he stood to the side of the sound guys.

"You ready to see dad perform?" she lifted his ear protection off his ears to ask the question.

He turned around to her. "Yeah," he smiled the same dimpled smile Garrett always gave her. "Thanks for coming out here tonight, mom."

Freakin' melted her heart. They'd never watched the show from the audience. She'd always been too scared, because Black Friday frequently told their fans to form a mosh pit, there were usually circle pits, and she was flat out worried both of them would get tousled by the massive amounts of bodies that crammed themselves into the general admission area of their concerts. Tonight though, EJ had looked much older than his six years when he'd told her he *wasn't a baby like his brother* anymore, and he wanted to watch his dad and uncles perform from the audience.

Telling Garrett had been the only thing she could think to do. They didn't travel with security and it was rare they told their children *no* when it came to a request involving the other parent. The compromise had been the two of them watching the show from the sound engineer's booth, located at the back of the general admission area. It was always gated off, and usually security stood outside to keep the public from bothering the guys trying to do their job. Shell kept their youngest son backstage with her and Jared's daughter. Hannah hoped the two wouldn't wear her friend out; she owed her friend an adult night out with her hubby for keeping the kids.

The lights dimmed and she dutifully pushed his ear protection down over his head, waiting for the guys to make an appearance. The crowd was a palpable force she could feel all the way from her feet up to her ears. They were excited, chanting *Reaper* and *Black Friday* in succession. Music played, but it was a well-known song by an older band, this told the guys backstage they had a few minutes to make their way up. It was the last quiet time they had before going to perform.

She found herself clapping along with the rest of the crowd, holding her breath, waiting to see Reaper in all his glory, waiting to hear the first beats of the song she knew they started with. EJ clapped his hands too, yelling along with the thousands of other voices. She wondered if knew exactly why he was yelling and then she decided it didn't matter.

The beginning drum beats hit as well as the guitar chords, and she felt the excitement well up in her chest. The crowd, and her, knew Reaper would be coming from stage left; he always came from stage left. Hannah knew when people saw him, because she could hear the immediate screams of feminine origins. That was when she saw him too.

Dear God, her husband was hot. She'd never seen a concert of his like this before, and wondered why she'd never made the time as she watched him run over, and jump on the riser beside Jared. The crowd screamed their approval and he nodded, running his hand over his bald head, before he opened his mouth and let forth the sexiest growl she'd ever heard in her life.

"Dad!" EJ screamed, waving from where she held him tightly.

She grinned, knowing Garrett couldn't see him, but it made her happy just the same. Pushing her hair back from her face, she sighed deeply as she watched Reaper run around on stage.

He'd started shaving his head over the summer when it'd gotten *too hot for hair*, and while it had taken a while to grow on her, just like his long hair had, she now loved it. With his strong jawline, dimples, and the five o'clock shadow he perpetually sported now, it made him look manlier if that was even possible.

"C'mon Atlanta!" he yelled, holding them in the palm of his hand. She listened as he sang the first part of the lyrics and then held the mic to the crowd, grinning when both she and EJ sung the words.

Her eyes followed him as he bent down on the riser to be closer to the kids in front. She knew from experience the move sometimes hurt his knees. Regardless of how hot he was, he was on the other side of thirty and she constantly reminded him people would understand if he didn't move like he was twenty anymore. But he couldn't help it, the adrenaline coursed through his body from opening to end, and then sometimes even afterwards. Sometimes….when they made sure the boys were tucked into their beds….she became his groupie all over again. Something, Hannah would definitely enjoy doing tonight. She breathed loudly as he took his jacket off.

Good God, he shouldn't look this hot, she told herself. After almost eight years together, she shouldn't want him this much. That was what she told herself every day, but it was the truth she still wanted him just as bad today as she had when they first met.

The music stopped and Garrett grabbed a mic stand. "How're you doing tonight Atlanta?" He asked, waiting for them to answer back before he kept speaking.

She could see sweat rolling off his body, on the screen that backed up the band. The coloring caused his tattoos to stand out, and the stubble was visible to every eye in the arena. She wanted to lean over and thank the video guy for keeping the camera on the hotness who'd given her a different last name.

"Thank you for coming out on this Wednesday night to the rock show. How many of you are calling into work tomorrow?"

Hannah giggled as she saw almost every hand go up in the arena.

"I would too, no shit," he laughed. "I'd be like fuck

this, I'm too hungover."

The crowd roared with enthusiasm.

"Mom," EJ yelled at her, his eyes wide. "Dad's cussin' again."

"I know," she cringed. "But you remember what we said about him being on stage? It's an act. These people expect him to say these things."

"But at home he has to put money in the curse jar?" her son questioned.

At least while you and your brother are awake. "Right," she hugged his little body tightly to her.

"I'm looking out over this crowd and I see some young kids in the pit," Reaper walked closer to the people, lifting his sunglasses up slightly. "How old are you?" he pointed to a kid on a man's shoulders. "Seven?" he questioned as they spoke back and forth. "Dad you're doin' a fuckin' good job. We've got to introduce these kids young. My son's out in the audience with my gorgeous wife tonight. Normally I'd bring her on stage to sing a little later, but she's on mommy duty," he pointed to the back where they stood.

The spotlight came on them, and she told EJ to wave. The crowd was deafening as they caught a glimpse of the child everyone who knew him called *Little Reaper*.

"This is the first time my son's watched from the audience, so I'm gonna hope we give him a good time, and since this is when I'd normally bring Harmony up to sing with me, we're gonna do something a little different. You know I have two boys, but EJ, my oldest is the one who's really into music. He loves our old stuff, like I'm talking first album old stuff, and he always asks that I play this next song for him. We'd never, ever done this song live before, but I want to make this night a memorable for me as I hope it is for him."

He rattled off the name of a seriously deep cut from their first album and EJ started screaming, jumping up and down as Hannah held onto him tightly. "Your dad's doing that for you," she kissed him on the cheek.

"So this one goes out to my mini-me, love you buddy."

Hannah knew without a doubt that tonight, if her husband wanted a groupie, then a groupie was what she'd be. Nothing made her fall in love with him more, than seeing him be a good dad and an even hotter entertainer. She truly was the luckiest woman in the world because she'd always be Reaper's Girl.

Connect with Laramie

Website:
www.laramiebriscoe.net

Facebook:
facebook.com/AuthorLaramieBriscoe

Twitter:
twitter.com/LaramieBriscoe

Pinterest:
pinterest.com/laramiebriscoe

Instagram:
instagram.com/laramie_briscoe

Substance B:
substance-b.com/LaramieBriscoe.html

Mailing List:
http://eepurl.com/Fi4N9

Email:
Laramie@laramiebriscoe.com

Sneak Peek of Trick

Releasing January 13, 2017

Chapter One

Hadley

"You're his last hope."

Rebecca, the director of The Companion Program lays it on thick, and I'm doing my best to be open-minded, but what she's told me is has me doubting my decisions. "He's a felon?" I rub my forehead with the heel of my hand, hoping to relieve some of the pressure that's built behind my eyes. This is a big decision.

"He's been a felon before," she clarifies. "This charge has escalated because of his past, but I assure you – he is a changed man."

Am I crazy for even considering this? On one hand, I think so, on the other, I try to see the best in everyone and I know it's possible to change. Look at what I've done for myself in the past two years. Who am I to judge? "What did he do?"

"It's a vandalism charge. That's all I'm allowed to say, but if he can't be matched with a child to perform his community service hours, he's going to go to jail. The time in jail will be exacerbated by his previous charges, and he's trying to build a business, trying to re-build a life. I've gotten to know him," the older woman gives me a sympathetic smile. "He's not a bad man. Put himself in bad situations and reacted badly? Sure. But bottom line is if she was my child, I'd trust him with her."

I look over at my daughter, Riley, and wonder if I'm doing the right thing. In my heart I know I am. She's been devastated; we've been devastated since my husband walked out on us. He left what I thought was a good and solid marriage to move in with a woman who didn't care he had a child. Children aren't her thing. That's left Riles without the guidance of a male figure and she's been withdrawn since the separation began. It only got worse as the divorce dragged on. When it was final, we were appointed a court counselor, and the counselor suggested I contact The Companion Care program which leads me to where I am now.

"You swear you'd trust your child with him?"

"I would," she tells me, reaching out to grip my hand. The contact is enough to startle me. For the months leading up to the separation, my husband and I never touched, and since then it's been me and her. It's foreign to feel someone else's skin against mine now. Regardless of their gender or age. When you aren't touched for long periods of time, it's a shock to the system when it's being reintroduced.

"Can I be there? I don't want her to feel uncomfortable, and I'd like to know who he is myself. She and I have been a team for a while now, and I'd like for us to do this together."

She balks for the first time and it gives me pause. I wonder why she's giving me a look of warning. What's she hiding?

"I'll allow it, but I'm going to be honest with you," she stops and sighs. "Patrick Tennyson is a gorgeous man. If I wasn't happily married for the past twenty-five years, I would make a pass at him – age difference be damned."

I laugh despite myself.

"The other two kids we've paired him with have been a problem because their mothers have made it difficult for Patrick."

Oh, I understand now. I hold my hands up. "That won't be a problem with me. I'm a single mom who works a full-time job, goes home does a part-time job, and takes care of her child. I'm not looking for a relationship now, or five years from now. I'm just trying to live my life and put food on our table." As God as my witness those words are true. I'm still trying to get over the anger, despair, and grief I feel having lost my eight-year marriage. That's not to say I'm not open to something happening for me in the future, but I'll never chase it.

"Okay Hadley, we'll set up the meeting, and we'll expect good results."

I stand, holding out my hand to the director. I can feel hope and optimism for the first time since my ex-husband left. Maybe this man can help me reach Riley, maybe he can help her understand not all mean leave, and maybe if she believes then so can I.

Trick

"How is this one going to be different than the rest?"

I kick my long legs out in front of me, trying not to make too much noise as the steel-toes of my boots meet the metal of the desk in front of me. Regardless of what other people think about me, I would prefer to blend into the background. I don't really want to make a spectacle of myself. I've been told the way I carry myself doesn't allow me to blend into the background, but I am who I am and I refuse to let people screw me around.

Matthew, my probation officer, God bless his soul is flipping through some paperwork. "They swear this woman isn't interested in finding a man, and apparently the little girl needs someone who can help her. The name's Riley."

"What's wrong with her?" I lean forward, keeping my arms tucked tightly across my chest, hands in my armpits. As a kid, I had a bad habit of talking with my hands. My dad didn't like it, so I learned to keep them close to my body.

He's going over the info sheet. "Looks like the dad slash husband walked out on them, and he isn't interested in being a father to Riley anymore. She's withdrawn and the mother is worried. Hadley, the mother has requested she be there for at least the first few sessions."

Any mother who gave a damn about her kid would,

but that makes me nervous. "I can't fault her for wanting to be there, but damn what if she turns into another one? I can't go to jail, the fucking shop is booked solid for the next three months. I've finally got all my shit figured out."

"I know, and don't think I'm not sympathetic to your plight, Patrick."

"Oh kiss my ass, you know I hate when people call me by my given name."

Matthew glares. "There does need to be some semblance of professionalism here, no matter how much I like you and feel as if you're doing great things."

Fuck me, I roll my neck, already feeling a tension headache starting to form. I've already wasted too much time today. "Just set it up and let me know what time I need to be there."

It's time to pay my debt to society. To try and right the wrongs I caused as an angry young adult who had nobody to shape me into the man I have become. The vandalism charge? That's bullshit and another story for another day. I pull my phone out of the pocket of my well-worn jeans. Shit it's already two pm. I'm gonna be at the shop late tonight.

"Tomorrow, nine am. They want to get this show on the road, and the quicker you start, the quicker your hours will accumulate."

Whatever. "See ya in two weeks," I tell him, referencing my next parole check in.

I have work to do, and it looks like I have a little girl to meet tomorrow. As I step out into the bright sunshine, I put on my aviators and hope like hell traffic isn't bad as I make my way back across the bridge to my side of town. The side where I'm comfortable – where people have rough edges and good hearts. My edges have sometimes been razor sharp and it's time to dull them – anger and resentment has gotten me nowhere but serving almost a thousand hours of community service.

Growing up sucks, especially when you realize all the bad shit you've done to yourself, to spite yourself. I've never shied away from taking responsibility and I'll take this the way I have everything else, but damn if it's not coming at the worst possible time for me personally.

I start my bike and ease into afternoon traffic. Time to get to work.

A loud noise wakes me from a sleep so deep I'm pretty fucking sure I was dead. It's this annoying beep – constant and getting louder by the second. I reach out, slapping my hand against my cell phone, but it keeps going off. Why did I set the alarm? I wrack my brain, trying to figure out why in the hell I had to get up so early today. I was in the shop until almost four in the morning, but I made sure to set my alarm. Why? The reason is right on the edge of my periphery of a memory but it's not clicking.

Suddenly I set up, knowing exactly where I should be today, what I should be doing. The sinking feeling is already taking up residence in my stomach.

"Son of a fucking bitch," I grab the phone, squinting

to see what time it is. Eight fifty-five. "Shit!"

It's inevitable I'm going to be late as hell for my first day. What a way to make a good impression. Quickly I put on the nearest clothes, a jacket, run my hand through my short hair, and head out. Effort counts right? Because I'm about to put forth the most effort I ever have. This shit has to work.

Sneak Peek of Renegade
Releasing March 9th, 2017

Chapter One
Whitney

"Ryan, I'm tellin' you, I need my hair pulled, I need a red handprint across my ass, I need someone paying attention to my nipples, a dick in my treasure cove. I need it all."

Drunk. I am drunk. Like way past the legal limit – otherwise I wouldn't be sitting here spilling all of my secrets to my baby brother's best friend. The baby brother that had been totally unplanned by my parents. Ten years my junior, baby brother. He and Ryan are the same age; twenty-five to my thirty-five. Makes me feel so much older, just thinking about it. Not only by age, but by life experience too. And dear Lord, I think I sound like Julia Sugarbaker. I'm three sheets to the wind, and nobody stopped me.

I see him try to suppress a grin as he brings his bottle of beer up to his lips, taking a nice long pull off of it. I am mesmerized by the way his throat muscles move when he swallows, pushing the liquid down his throat. No denying he's a man. The palm of his hand completely covers the label on the bottle, the one drink he takes, almost drains half the bottle. For a second he focuses on my face, squinting as he watches me. "How many of those have you had to drink?" He points the neck of his bottle to the wine glass in my hand.

His voice is as smooth as the wine I swirl in my glass. I tilt my head to the side, realizing that the whole room tilts too. Counting back, I try to think how many I had before he took the seat next to mine, and I can't remember. "Five or six?" I ask him, like he should know.

"You think maybe it's time you quit for the night?" He gently tries to take what I have left away from me.

His fingers are soft as they try to pry my fingers from around the stem, but I resist his attempts, and pull it closer to my body. I'm like a two-year-old with her blankie. This glass of wine is my security and nobody's taking it away from me.

"Quit?" I ask, and run my tongue over my dry lips, trying to make them so that they can speak easier. "Quitting is not something I do. That's what my ex-husband did. My mama did. That's what my former boss did," I shake my head, and try to stand up on four-inch stilettos. He reaches out and grabs my elbow, steadying me, being a rock when I haven't had one in a very long time. "Whitney Trumbolt is not a fuckin' quitter."

I can see Ryan try again to keep the smile from his face. The corners of his lips twitch, and it pisses me off. Not because I'm mad, but because he thinks it's funny.

He thinks this is a joke, and it's my life. The life I've been trying so desperately to get out from under or save. I'm not sure which yet. All I know is I haven't been living.

"You think this is funny?" I take another drink from my wine glass. It's a big one this time, I drain it down.

"No, Whit, I think you're having a bad night." His tone is one someone would use with a kindergartner, talking them down from a temper tantrum. It pisses me off too.

A bad night? Try a bad decade. If I could do anything, it would go back to the night I turned twenty-five, and be the age that Ryan is again. I would do so many things different, I would change so much about the choices that I made back then. "You know nothing about me, other than the fact that I'm Tank's sister."

He grabs me by the wrist, locking his fingers around the skin and bone. I never realized until this moment how much bigger he is than me. Never really paid any kind of attention to it – oh I've paid attention to him off and on through-out the years, but never like this.

Ryan "Renegade" Kepler rises to his full height, towering over me as I do my best to keep my footing and ignore the way my skin tingles where he is gripping my wrist. He leans in close – so close I can feel his breath on my skin.

"I know a lot of things about you that you don't think I know."

His voice is hard and soft at the same time. I close my eyes to savor it. This is the closest I've been to a man in a very long time. My body is at attention, as is my libido.

"I know that you love your mama's fried chicken, your grandmother's homemade mac and cheese, Alabama football, and Dale Earnhardt Jr. I know that you have a soft heart. Hallmark movies make you cry, you pick up strays on the side of the road, and you always buy that homeless man near the Starbucks a morning coffee," he tells me.

I'm wrapped up in his voice, in the things he does know about me. Things I never knew that he'd paid attention to. I'm swaying, but it's because his voice is doing weird things to my equilibrium. His other hand wraps around my hip and I can feel the heat of his body through the material of my skirt.

"I know that your ex-husband was a piece of shit. I know that your ex-boss didn't know what the hell to do with the creative genius that is your mind, and I know that your mama will never forgive you for giving up pageants, but she'll never forgive herself for pushing you that damn hard," he stops and pulls back, giving me his eyes and face to stare at.

Our eyes meet and I realize with clarity that I'm breathing hard, hard enough that it feels as if I've run a marathon.

"You wanna know what else I know?" The question is asked in a way that says he's not sure if he wants to answer tonight. There's a string of awareness stretched between us, and it's pulling me closer.

I'm captivated by the way the dim lights of the bar make his brown eyes seem darker, I'm enthralled by the fact that it looks like it's been a few days since he shaved, and I'm even more fascinated by the cut he has on his cheek. He and Tank went out on a call last night, and I can't help but wonder if that cut is the result of it. I shake my head and then nod, because I do want to find out what else he knows. I step forward, put my arms around his neck, and lean up so that now I'm the one in his ear. "Tell me what else you know."

I see him look around the bar, checking to make sure that we're not being paid any attention to. He bends with his knees and grips my ass cheeks in his hands. "I know I'm the one that can put my dick in that treasure cove. I know I'm the one that can pull that hair, I can pull on those nipples, and I can smack that ass. The question is – will you let me?"

It's not a question I can say no to. The way the air cackles between us, and the alcohol I've consumed. There's not any way that I can say no nor is there any desire on my part to deny it. I've denied myself a lot of things in this life, and this right here, is not something that I want to brush off.

"Yes," I breath out….adding on a "please."

"Oh baby, you don't have to beg. I'll do whatever you need me to," Ryan says as I find my hand in his and stumble to keep up as he pulls us out of the bar.

In mere minutes I'm in his truck, and we're headed towards my house. I will myself not to pass out, because for the first time in years, I want to be here and present for this experience that's about to happen. I want to remember every damn detail. If it's only going to be for this one night, I don't want to miss a thing.